UNLOCKING HER SURGEON'S HEART

BY
FIONA LOWE

First published in Great Britain 2015
by Mills & Boon, an imprint of Harlequin (UK) Limited,
Large Print edition 2016
Eton House, 18-24 Paradise Road,
Richmond, Surrey, TW9 1SR

Special thanks and acknowledgement are given to Fiona Lowe for her contribution to the Midwives On-Call series.

ISBN: 978-0-263-26068-7

Harlequin (UK) Limited's policy is to use papers that are natural, renewable and recyclable products and made from wood grown in sustainable forests. The logging and manufacturing processes conform to the legal environmental regulations of the country of origin.

Printed and bound in Great Britain
by CPI Antony Rowe, Chippenham, Wiltshire

To my fellow Mills & Boon Medical Romance authors.
You're all amazing and talented women.
Thank you for the support, the laughs and the fun times when we were lucky enough to meet in person.

Always an avid reader, **Fiona Lowe** decided to combine her love of romance with her interest in all things medical, so writing Mills & Boon Medical Romance was an obvious choice! She lives in a seaside town in southern Australia, where she juggles writing, reading, working and raising two gorgeous sons with the support of her own real-life hero!

Books by Fiona Lowe

Mills & Boon Medical Romance

Miracle: Twin Babies
Her Brooding Italian Surgeon
The Most Magical Gift of All
Single Dad's Triple Trouble
Career Girl in the Country
Sydney Harbour Hospital: Tom's Redemption
Letting Go with Dr Rodriguez
Newborn Baby For Christmas
Gold Coast Angels: Bundle of Trouble

Visit the Author Profile page at millsandboon.co.uk for more titles.

Praise for Fiona Lowe

'Pure Fiona Lowe brilliance...emotional, heartwarming and brought me to tears!'

—*Contemporary Romance Reviews* on *Gold Coast Angels: Bundle of Trouble*

'Fiona Lowe is a genius at writing multilayered storylines that mesh seamlessly with each other to create a beautifully emotional read.'

—*HarlequinJunkie* on *Letting Go with Dr Rodriguez*

MIDWIVES ON-CALL

Midwives, mothers and babies—
lives changing for ever...!

Enter the magical world of the Melbourne Maternity Unit and the exceptional midwives there, delivering tiny bundles of joy on a daily basis. Now it's time to find a happy-ever-after of their own...

Just One Night? by Carol Marinelli
Gorgeous Greek doctor Alessi Manos is determined to charm the beautiful yet frosty Isla Delamere... but can he melt this ice queen's heart?

Meant-To-Be Family by Marion Lennox
When Dr Oliver Evans's estranged wife, Emily, crashes back into his life, old passions are reignited. But brilliant Dr Evans is in for a surprise... Emily has two foster children!

Always the Midwife by Alison Roberts
Midwife Sophia Toulson and hard-working paramedic Aiden Harrison share an explosive attraction...but will they overcome their tragic pasts and take a chance on love?

Midwife's Baby Bump by Susanne Hampton
Hotshot surgeon Tristan Hamilton's passionate night with pretty student midwife Flick has unexpected consequences!

Midwife...to Mum! by Sue MacKay
Free-spirited locum midwife Ally Parker meets top GP and gorgeous single dad Flynn Reynolds. Is she finally ready to settle down with a family of her own?

His Best Friend's Baby by Susan Carlisle
When beautiful redhead Phoebe Taylor turns up on ex-army medic Ryan Matthews's doorstep there's only one thing keeping them apart: she's his best friend's widow...and eight months pregnant!

Unlocking Her Surgeon's Heart by Fiona Lowe
Brooding city surgeon Noah Jackson meets compassionate Outback midwife Lilia Cartwright. Could Lilia be the key to Noah's locked-away heart?

Her Playboy's Secret by Tina Beckett
Renowned English obstetrician Darcie Green might think playboy Lucas Elliot is nothing but trouble— but is there more to this gorgeous doc than meets the eye?

Experience heartwarming emotion and pulse-racing drama in *Midwives On-Call* this sensational eight-book continuity from Mills & Boon Medical Romance

These books are also available in eBook format from millsandboon.co.uk

CHAPTER ONE

'WANT TO CLOSE?'

Noah Jackson, senior surgical registrar at the Melbourne Victoria Hospital, smiled behind his mask as he watched the answer to his question glow in the eyes of his surgical intern.

'Do I support The Westies?' Rick Stewart quipped, his eyes alight with enthusiasm. His loyalty to the struggling Australian Rules football team was legendary amongst the staff, who teased him mercilessly.

'For Mrs Levatti's sake, you need to close better than your team plays,' Noah said, knowing full well Rick was more than capable.

There'd be no way he'd allow him to stitch up his patient unless he was three levels above competent. The guy reminded him of himself back in the day when he'd been an intern—keen, driven and determined to succeed.

'Thanks, team.' Noah stepped back from the operating table and stripped off his gloves, his mind already a long way from work. 'It's been a huge week and I've got the weekend off.'

'Lucky bastard,' muttered Ed Yang, the anaesthetist. 'I'm on call for the entire weekend.'

Noah had little sympathy. 'It's my first weekend off in over a month and I'm starting it at the Rooftop with one of their boutique beers.'

'I might see you there later,' Lizzy said casually.

The scout nurse's come-hither green eyes sparkled at him, reminding him of a previous good time together. 'Everyone's welcome,' he added, not wanting to tie himself down to anyone or anything. 'I'll be there until late.'

He strode out and headed purposefully towards the change rooms, savouring freedom. Anticipation bubbled in him as he thought about his hard-earned weekend of sleeping in, cycling along the Yarra, catching a game at the MCG, eating at his favourite café, and finally seeing the French film everyone was talking about. God, he loved Melbourne in the spring and everything that it offered.

'Noah.'

The familiar deep voice behind him made him reluctantly slow and he turned to face the distinguished man the nursing staff called the silver fox.

'You got a minute?' Daniel Serpell asked.

No. But that wasn't a word an intern or registrar ever said to the chief of surgery. 'Sure.'

The older man nodded slowly. 'Great job on that lacerated liver on Tuesday. Impressive.'

The unexpected praise from the hard taskmaster made Noah want to punch the air. 'Thanks. It was touch and go for a bit and we almost put the blood bank into deficit but we won.'

'No one in this hospital has any doubt about your surgical abilities, Noah.'

Something about the way his boss hit the word *surgical* made Noah uneasy. 'That's a good thing, right?'

'There are nine areas of competency to satisfy the Royal Australasian College of Surgeons.'

Noah was familiar with every single one of them now that his final surgical exams were only a few months away. 'Got them all covered, Prof.'

'You might think that, Noah, but others don't agree.' He reached inside his jacket and produced a white envelope with Noah's name printed on it.

'What's this?'

'Your solution to competency number two.'

'I don't follow.'

The prof sighed. 'Noah, I can't fault you on technical skills and I'd trust you to operate on me, my wife and my family. You're talented with your patients when they're asleep but we've had complaints from your dealings with them when they're awake.' He cleared his throat. 'We've also had complaints from staff.'

Noah's gut clenched so tight it burned and the envelope in his hand suddenly developed a crushing weight. 'Is this an official warning?'

'No, not at all,' the prof said genially. 'I'm on your side and this is the solution to your problem.'

'I didn't know I had a problem,' he said, not able to hide his defensiveness.

The professor raised a brow. 'And after this, I hope you won't have one either.'

'You're sending me on a communications course?' The idea of sitting around in a circle with a group of strangers and talking about feelings appalled him.

'Everything you need to know is in the envelope. Just make sure you're ready to start at eight o'clock on Monday morning.' He clapped a hand on Noah's shoulder. 'Enjoy your weekend off.'

As his boss walked away, Noah's anxiety ramped up ten notches and the pristine, white envelope now ticked like an unexploded bomb. Not wanting to read it in public, he walked quickly to the doctors' lounge, thankfully finding it empty. He ripped open the envelope and scanned the brief letter.

Dear Dr Jackson

Your four-week rotation at the Turraburra Medical Clinic commences on Monday,

August 17th at eight a.m. Accommodation, if required, is provided at the doctor's flat located on Nautalis Parade. Collect the key from the real estate agent in Williams Street before noon, Saturday. See the enclosed map and tourist information, which we hope will be of assistance to you.

Enjoy your rotation in Turraburra—the sapphire of South Gippsland.

Nancy Beveridge
Surgical Trainee Placement Officer.

No. No way. Noah's intake of breath was so sharp it made him cough. This could *not* be happening. They couldn't do this to him. Not now. Suddenly, the idea of a communications course seemed positively fun.

Relax. You must have read it wrong. Fighting the red heat of rage that was frantically duelling with disbelief, he slowly reread the letter, desperately hoping he'd misunderstood its message. As his eyes scrolled left to right and he slowed his mind down to read each and every word, it made no difference. The grim message the black and white letters told didn't change.

He was being exiled—sent rural—and the timing couldn't be worse. In fact, it totally sucked. Big time. He had less than six months before he sat his final surgical examinations and now more than ever his place was at the Victoria. He should be here, doing cutting-edge surgery, observing the latest technology, attending tutorials and studying. Always studying. He should *not* be stuck in a country clinic day in, day out, listening to the ramblings of patients with chronic health issues that surgery couldn't solve.

General practice. A shudder ran through him at the thought. There was a reason he'd aimed high and fought for his hard-earned place in the surgical programme, and a large part of it was to avoid the mundane routine of being a GP. He had no desire at all to have a long and ongoing connection with patients or get to know their families or be introduced to their dogs. This was blatantly unfair. Why the hell had he been singled out?

Damn it, none of the other surgical registrars had been asked to do this.

A vague memory of Oliver Evans bawling him out months ago flickered across his mind but surely that had nothing to do with this. Consultants yelled at registrars from time to time—usually during moments of high stress when the odds were stacked against them and everyone was battling to save a patient's life. Heated words were exchanged, a lot of swearing went down but at the end of the day it was forgotten and all was forgiven. It was all part of the cut and thrust of hospital life.

Logic immediately penetrated his incredulity. The prof had asked him to teach a workshop to the new interns in less than two weeks so this Turraburra couldn't be too far away from downtown Melbourne. Maybe he was just being sent to the growth corridor—the far-flung edges of the ever-growing city, the outer, outer 'burbs. That wouldn't be too bad. A bit of commuting wouldn't kill him and he could listen to his training podcasts on the drive there and back each day.

Feeling more positive, he squinted at the dot on the map.

His expletive rent the air, staining it blue. He'd been banished to the back of beyond.

Lilia Cartwright, never Lil and always Lily to her friends, stood on a whitewashed dock in the ever-brightening, early morning light. She stared out towards the horizon, welcoming the sting of salt against her cheeks, the wind in her hair, and she smiled. 'New day, Chippy,' she said to her tan and white greyhound who stared up at her with enormous, brown, soulful eyes. 'Come on, mate, look a bit more excited. After this walk, you'll have another day ahead of you of lazing about and being cuddled.'

Chippy tugged on his leash as he did every morning when they stood on the dock, always anxious to get back indoors. Back to safety.

Lily loved the outdoors but she understood only too well Chippy's need for safe places. Given his experiences during the first two years of his life, she didn't begrudge him one little bit, but she was starting to think she might need a second dog to go running with to keep fit. Walking with Chippy hardly constituted exercise because she never broke a sweat.

Turning away from the aquamarine sea, she walked towards the Turraburra Medical Centre. In the grounds of the small bush nursing hospital and nursing home, the glorious bluestone building had started life a hundred and thirty years ago as the original doctor's house. Now, fully restored, it was a modern clinic. She particularly loved her annexe—the midwifery clinic and birth centre. Although it was part of the medical centre, it had a separate entrance so her healthy, pregnant clients didn't have to sit in a waiting room full of coughing and hacking sick people. It had been one of the best days of her career when the Melbourne Midwifery Clinic had responded to her grant application and incorporated Turraburra into their outreach programme for rural and isolated women.

The clinic was her baby and she'd taken a lot of time and effort in choosing the soothing, pastel paint and the welcoming décor. She wanted it to feel less like a sterile clinic and far more like visiting someone's home. In a way, given that she'd put so much of herself into the project, the pregnant women and their families were visiting her home.

At first glance, the birthing suite looked like a room in a four-star hotel complete with a queen-sized bed, side tables, lounge chairs, television, bar fridge and a roomy bathroom. On closer inspection, though, it had all the important features found in any hospital room. Oxygen, suction and nitrous oxide outlets were discreetly incorporated in the wall whilst other medical equipment was stored in a cupboard that looked like a wardrobe and it was only brought out when required.

The birth centre didn't cater for high-risk pregnancies—those women were referred to Melbourne, where they could receive the high-tech level of care required for a safe, happy and healthy outcome for mother and baby. The Turraburra women who were deemed to be at a low risk of pregnancy and childbirth complications gave birth here, close to their homes and families. For Lily it was an honour to be part of the birth and to bring a new life into the world.

As Turraburra was a small town, it didn't stop there either. In the three years since she'd returned home and taken on the position of the town's midwife, she'd not only delivered a lot of babies, she'd also attended a lot of children's birthday parties. She loved watching the babies grow up and she could hardly believe that those first babies she'd delivered were now close to starting three-year-old kinder. As her involvement with the babies and children was as close as she was ever likely to get to having a family of her own, she treasured it even more.

Lily stepped into the main part of the clinic and automatically said, 'Morning, Karen,' before she realised the receptionist wasn't behind her desk. Karen's absence reminded her that a new doctor was starting today. Sadly, since the retirement of their beloved Dr Jameson two years ago, this wasn't an uncommon occurrence. She remembered the fuss they'd all made of the first new doctor to arrive in town—ever hopeful he'd be staying for years to come—but he'd left after three months. Seven other doctors had followed in a two-year period and all of the staff, including herself, had become a bit blasé about new arrivals. The gloss had long faded from their hope that *this one* might actually stay for the long term and grand welcoming gestures had fallen by the wayside.

Turraburra, like so many rural towns in Australia, lacked a permanent doctor. It did, however, have more than its fair share of overseas and Australian general practitioner trainees as well as numerous medical students. All of them passed through the clinic and hospital on short stays so they could tick their obligatory rural rotation off their list before hot-footing it back to Melbourne or Sydney or any other major capital city.

The cultural identity that to be Australian was to be at one with the bush was a myth. Australia was the most urbanised country in the world and most people wanted to be a stone's throw from a big city and all the conveniences that offered. Lily didn't agree. She loved Turraburra and it would take a major catastrophe for her to ever live in Melbourne again. She still bore the scars from her last attempt.

Some of the doctors who came to Turraburra were brilliant and the town begged them to stay longer, while others were happily farewelled with a collective sigh of relief and a long slug of fortifying beer or wine at the end of their rotation. Lily had been so busy over the weekend, delivering two babies, that she hadn't had time to open the email she'd received late on Friday with the information about 'doctor number nine'. She wondered if nine was going to be Turraburra's lucky number.

Chippy frantically tugged at his leash again. 'Yes, I know, we're here. Hang on a second.' She bent down and slid her hand under his wide silver and indigo decorative collar that one of the patients had made for him. It was elegant and had an air of Russian royalty about it, showing off his long and graceful neck. She released the clip from the leash and with far more enthusiasm than he ever showed on a walk, Chippy raced to his large, padded basket in the waiting room and curled up with a contented sigh.

He was the clinic's companion dog and all the patients from the tiny tots to the ninety-year-olds loved and adored him. He basked in the daily stroking and cuddles and Lily hoped his hours of being cosseted went some way towards healing the pain of his early life at the hands of a disreputable greyhound racer. She stroked his long nose. 'You have fun today and I'll see you tonight.'

Chippy smiled in the way only greyhounds can.

She crossed the waiting room and was collecting her mail from her pigeonhole when she heard, 'What the hell is that thing doing in here?'

She flinched at the raised, curt male voice and knew that Chippy would be shivering in his basket. Clutching her folders to her chest like a shield, she marched back into the waiting room. A tall guy with indecently glossy brown hair stood in the middle of the waiting room.

Two things instantly told her he was from out of town. Number one: she'd never met him. Number two: he was wearing a crisp white shirt with a tie that looked to be silk. It sat at his taut, freshly shaven throat in a wide Windsor knot that fitted perfectly against the collar with no hint of a gap or a glimpse of a top button. The tie was red and it contrasted dramatically with the dark grey pin-striped suit.

No one in Turraburra ever wore a suit unless they were attending a funeral, and even then no man in the district ever looked this neat, tailored, or gorgeous in a suit.

Gorgeous or not, his loud and curt voice had Chippy shrinking into his basket with fear. Her spine stiffened. Working hard at keeping calm and showing no fear, she said quietly, 'I could ask you the same question.'

His chestnut-brown brows arrowed down fast into a dark V, forming a deep crease above the bridge of his nose. He looked taken aback. 'I'm *supposed* to be here.'

She thought she heard him mutter, 'Worse

luck,' as he quickly shoved a large hand with neatly trimmed nails out towards her. The abrupt action had every part of her urging her to step back for safety. *Stop it. It's okay.* With great effort she glued her feet to the floor and stayed put but she didn't take her gaze off his wide hand.

'Noah Jackson,' he said briskly. 'Senior surgical registrar at Melbourne Victoria Hospital.'

She instantly recognised his name. She'd rung her friend Ally about him when she'd first heard he was meant to be coming but Ally had felt that there was no way he'd ever come to work at Turraburra. At the time it had made total sense because no surgery was done here anymore, and she'd thought there had just been a mistake. So why was he standing in the clinic waiting room, filling it with his impressive height and breadth?

She realised he was giving her an odd look and his hand was now hovering between them. Slowly, she let her right hand fall from across her chest. 'Lilia Cartwright. Midwife.'

His palm slid against hers—warm and smooth—and then his long, strong fingers gripped the back of her hand. It was a firm, fast, no-nonsense handshake and it was over quickly, but the memory of the pressure lingered on her skin. She didn't want to think about it. Not that it was awful, it was far from that, but the firm pressure of hands on her skin wasn't something she dwelled on. Ever.

She pulled her hand back across her chest and concentrated on why Noah Jackson was there. 'Has the Turraburra hospital board come into some money? Are they reopening the operating theatre?'

His full lips flattened into a grim line. 'I'm not that lucky.'

'Excuse me?'

'I haven't come here as a surgeon.'

His words punched the air with the pop and fizz of barely restrained politeness, which matched his tight expression. Was he upset? Perhaps he'd come to Turraburra for a funeral after all. Her eyes flicked over his suit and, despite not wanting to, she noticed how well it fitted his body. How his trousers highlighted his narrow hips and sat flat against his abdomen. How the tailored jacket emphasised his broad shoulders.

Not safe, Lily. She swallowed and found her voice. 'What have you come as, then?'

He threw out his left arm, gesticulating towards the door. 'I'm this poor excuse of a town's doctor for the next month.'

'No.' The word shot out automatically—deep and disbelieving—driven from her mouth in defence of her beloved town. In defence of the patients.

Turraburra needed a general practitioner, not a surgeon. The character traits required to become a surgeon—a driven personality, arrogance and high self-belief, along with viewing every patient in terms of 'cutting out the problem'—were so far removed from a perfect match for Turraburra that it was laughable. What on earth was going on at the Melbourne Victoria that made them send a surgical registrar to be a locum GP? Heaven help them all.

His shoulders, already square, vibrated with tension and his brown eyes flashed with flecks of gold. 'Believe me, Ms Cartwright,' he said coldly, 'if I had things my way, I wouldn't be seen dead working here, but the powers that be have other plans. Neither of us has a choice.'

His antagonism slammed into her like storm waves pounding against the pier. She acknowledged that she deserved some of his hostility because her heartfelt, shock-driven 'No' had been impolite and unwelcoming. It had unwittingly put in her a position she avoided—that of making men angry. When it came to men in general she worked hard at going through life very much under their radar. The less she was noticed the better, and she certainly didn't actively set out to make them angry.

She sucked in a breath. 'I'm just surprised the Melbourne Victoria's sent a surgeon to us, but, as you so succinctly pointed out, neither of us has a choice.' She forced herself to smile, but it felt tight around the edges. 'Welcome to Turraburra, Dr Jackson.'

He gave a half grunting, half huffing sound and swung his critical gaze back to Chippy. 'Get the dog out of here. It doesn't belong in a medical clinic.'

All her guilt about her own rudeness vanished and along with it her usual protective guard. 'Chippy is the clinic's therapy dog. He stays.'

Noah stared at the tall, willowy woman in front of him whose fingers had a death grip on a set of bright pink folders. Her pale cheeks had two bright spots of colour on them that matched her files and her sky-blue eyes sparked with the silver flash of a fencing foil. He was still smarting from her definite and decisive 'No'. He might not want to work in this godforsaken place but who was she to judge him before he'd even started? 'What the hell is a therapy dog?'

'He provides some normalcy in the clinic,' she said, her tone clipped.

'Normalcy?' He gave a harsh laugh, remembering his mother's struggle to maintain any semblance of a normal life after her diagnosis. Remembering all the hours they'd spent in numerous medical practices' waiting rooms, not dissimilar to this one, seeking a cure that had never come. 'This is a medical clinic. It exists for sick people so there's nothing normal about it. And talking about normal, that dog looks far from it.'

She pursed her lips and he noticed how they peaked in a very kissable bow before flushing a deep and enticing red. Usually, seeing something sexy like that on a woman was enough for him to turn on the charm but no way in hell was he was doing that with this prickly woman with the fault-finding gaze.

'Chippy's a greyhound,' she snapped. 'They're supposed to be svelte animals.'

'Is that what you call it?' His laugh came out in a snort. 'It looks anorexic to me and what's with the collar? Is he descended from the tsars?'

He knew he was being obnoxious but there was something about Lilia Cartwright and her holier-than-thou tone that brought out the worst in him. Or was it the fact he'd spent the night sleeping on the world's most uncomfortable bed and when he'd finally fallen asleep the harsh and incessant screeching of sulphur-crested cockatoos at dawn had woken him. God, he hated the country.

'Have you quite finished?' she said, her voice so cool he expected icicles to form on her ash-blonde hair. 'Chippy calms agitated patients and the elderly at the nursing home adore him. Some of them don't have anyone in their lives they can lavish affection on and Chippy is more than happy to be the recipient of that love. Medical studies have shown that a companion pet lowers blood pressure and eases emotional distress. Like I said, he absolutely stays.'

An irrational urge filled him to kick something and to kick it hard. He had the craziest feeling he was back in kindergarten and being timed out on the mat for bad behaviour. 'If there's even one complaint or one flea bite, the mutt goes.'

Her brows rose in a perfect arc of condescension. 'In relative terms, Dr Jackson, you're here for a blink of an eye. Chippy will far outstay you.'

The blink of an eye? Who was she kidding? 'I'm here for seven hundred and twenty *very* long hours.'

Her blue eyes rounded. 'You actually counted them?'

He shrugged. 'It seemed appropriate at three a.m. when the hiss of fighting possums wearing bovver boots on my roof kept me awake.'

She laughed and unexpected dimples appeared in her cheeks. For a brief moment he glimpsed what she might look like if she ever relaxed. It tempted him to join her in laughter but then her tension-filled aura slammed back in place, shutting out any attempts at a connection.

He crossed his arms. 'It wasn't funny.'

'I happen to know you could just have easily been kept awake by fighting possums in the leafy suburbs of Melbourne.'

Were they comrades-in-arms? Both victims of the vagaries of the Melbourne Victoria Hospital that had insisted on sending them to the back of beyond? A bubble of conciliation rose to the top of his dislike for her. 'So you've been forced down here too?'

She shook her head so quickly that her thick and tight French braid swung across her shoulder. 'Turraburra is my home. Melbourne was just a grimy pitstop I was forced to endure when I studied midwifery.'

He thought about his sun-filled apartment in leafy Kew, overlooking Yarra Bend Park. 'My Melbourne's not grimy.'

Again, one brow quirked up in disapproval. 'My Turraburra's not a poor excuse for a town.'

'Well, at least we agree on our disagreement.'

'Do you plan to be grumpy for the entire time you're here?'

Her directness both annoyed and amused him. 'Pretty much.'

One corner of her mouth twitched. 'I guess forewarned is forearmed.' She turned to go and then spun back. 'Oh, and a word to the wise, that is, of course, if you're capable of taking advice on board. I suggest you do things Karen's way. She's run this clinic for fifteen years and outstayed a myriad of medical staff.'

He bit off an acidic retort. He hadn't even met a patient yet but if this last fifteen minutes with Ms Lilia Cartwright, Midwife, was anything to go by, it was going to be a hellishly long and difficult seven hundred and nineteen hours and forty-five minutes in Turraburra.

CHAPTER TWO

'I'M HOME!' LILY CALLED loudly over the blare of the TV so her grandfather had a chance of hearing her.

A thin arm shot up above the top of the couch and waved at her. 'Marshmallow and I are watching re-runs of the doctor. Makes me realise you don't see many phone boxes around any more, do you?'

Lily kissed him affectionately on the top of his head and stroked the sleeping cat as Chippy settled across her grandfather's feet. 'Until the mobile phone reception improves, I think Turraburra's phone box is safe.'

'I just hope I'm still alive by the time the national broadband scheme's rolled out. The internet was so dodgy today it took me three goes before I could check my footy tipping site.'

'A definite tragedy,' she said wryly. Her grandfather loved all sports but at this time of year, with only a few games before the Australian Rules football finals started, he took it all very seriously. 'Did you get down to the community centre today?'

He grunted.

'Gramps?' A ripple of anxiety wove through her that he might have driven to the centre.

Just recently, due to some episodes of numbness in his feet, she'd reluctantly told him it wasn't safe for him to drive. Given how independent he was, he'd been seriously unhappy with that proclamation. It had taken quite some time to convince him but he'd finally seemed to come round and together they'd chosen a mobility scooter. Even at eighty-five, he'd insisted on getting a red one because everyone knew red went faster.

It was perfect for getting around Turraburra and, as she'd pointed out to him, he didn't drive out of town much anyway. But despite all the logic behind the decision, the 'gopher', as he called it, had stayed in the garage. Lily was waiting for him to get sick of walking everywhere and start using it.

'I took the gopher,' he said grumpily. 'Happy?'

'I'm happy you went to your class at the centre.'

'Well, I couldn't let Muriel loose on the computer. She'd muck up all the settings and, besides, it was my day to teach the oldies how to edit photos.'

She pressed her lips together so she didn't laugh, knowing from experience it didn't go down well. He might be in his eighties but his mind was as sharp as a tack and he was young at heart, even if his body was starting to fail him. She ached when she thought of how much he hated that. Losing the car had been a bitter blow.

The 'oldies' he referred to were a group of frail elderly folk from the retirement home. Many were younger than him and made him look positively spry. He was interested in anything and everything and involved in the life of the town. He loved keeping abreast of all the latest technology, loved his top-of-the-range digital camera and he kept busy every day. His passion and enthusiasm for life often made her feel that hers was pale and listless in comparison.

He was her family and she loved him dearly. She owed him more than she could ever repay.

'Muriel sent over a casserole for dinner,' he said, rising to his feet.

'That was kind of her.' Muriel and Gramps had a very close friendship and got along very well as long as she didn't touch his computer and he didn't try to organise her pantry into some semblance of order.

He walked towards the kitchen. 'She heard about the Hawker and De'Bortolli babies and knew you'd be tired. No new arrivals today?'

Lily thought about the tall, dark, ill-tempered surgical registrar who'd strode into her work world earlier in the day.

You forgot good looking.

No. Handsome belongs to someone who smiles.

Really? Trent smiled a lot and look how well that turned out.

She pulled her mind back fast from that thought

because the key to her mental health was to never think about Trent. Ever. 'A new doctor's arrived in town.'

His rheumy, pale blue eyes lit up. 'Male or female?'

'Sorry, Gramps. I know how you like to flirt with the female doctors but this one's a difficult bloke.' She couldn't stop the sigh that followed.

His face pulled down in a worried frown. 'Has he done something?'

Since the nightmare of her relationship with Trent, Gramps had been overprotective of her, and she moved to reassure him. 'No, nothing like that and I'm stronger now. I don't take any crap from anyone any more. I just know he's not a natural fit for Turraburra.'

'We're all entitled to one bad day—give the poor guy a minute to settle in. You and Karen will have him trained up in the Turraburra ways in no time flat.'

I wish. 'I'm not so sure about that, Gramps. In fact, the only thing I have any confidence about at all is that it's going to be a seriously long month.'

* * *

Noah stood on the town beach, gulping in great lungfuls of salt air like it was the last drop of oxygen on the planet. Not that he believed in any of that positive-ions nonsense but he was desperate to banish the scent of air freshener with a urine chaser from his nostrils. From his clothes. From his skin.

His heart rate thundered hard and fast like it did after a long run, only this time its pounding had nothing to do with exercise and everything to do with anxiety. Slowing his breathing, he pulled in some long, controlled deep breaths and shucked off the cloak of claustrophobia that had come out of nowhere, engulfing him ten minutes earlier. It had been years since something like that had happened and as a result he'd thought he'd conquered it, but all it had taken was two hours at the Turraburra nursing home. God, he hated this town.

He'd arrived at the clinic at eight to be told by the efficient Karen that Tuesday mornings meant rounds at the nursing home. He'd crossed the grounds of the hospital where the bright spring daffodils had mocked him with their cheery and optimistic colour. He hadn't felt the slightest bit cheery. The nurse in charge of the nursing home had given him a bundle of patient histories and a stack of drug sheets, which had immediately put paid to his plan of dashing in and dashing out.

Apparently, it had been three weeks since there'd been a doctor in Turraburra and his morning was consumed by that added complication. The first hour had passed relatively quickly by reviewing patient histories. After that, things had gone downhill fast as he'd examined each elderly patient. Men who'd once stood tall and strong now lay hunched, droop-faced and dribbling, rendered rigid by post-stroke muscle contractions. Women had stared at him with blank eyes—eyes that had reminded him of his mother's. Eyes that had told him they knew he could do nothing for them.

God, he hated that most. It was the reason he'd pursued surgery—at least when he operated on someone, he usually made a difference. He had the capacity to heal, to change lives, but today, in the nursing home, he hadn't been able to do any of that. All he'd been able to do had been to write prescriptions, suggest physiotherapy and recommend protein shakes. The memories of his mother's long and traumatic suffering had jeered at the idea that any of it added to their quality of life.

He'd just finished examining the last patient when the aroma of cabbage and beef, the scent of pure soap and lavender water and the pervading and cloying smell of liberally used air freshener had closed in on him. He'd suddenly found it very hard to breathe. He'd fled fast—desperate for fresh air—and in the process he'd rudely rejected the offer of tea and biscuits from the nurses.

He knew that wouldn't grant him any favours with the staff but he didn't care. In six hundred and ninety-six hours he'd be back in Melbourne. Pulling out his smartphone, he set up a countdown and called it T-zero. Now, whenever the town got to him, he didn't have to do the mental arithmetic, he could just open the app and easily see how many hours until he could walk away from Turraburra without a backward glance.

The fresh, salty air and the long, deep breaths had done the trick and, feeling back in control, he jogged up the beach steps. Sitting on the sea wall, he took off his shoes to empty them of sand.

'Yoo-hoo, Dr Jackson.'

He glanced up to see a line of cycling, fluoro-clad women—all who looked to be in their sixties—bearing down on him fast. The woman in front was waving enthusiastically but with a bicycle helmet on her head and sunglasses on her face he didn't recognise her.

He gave a quick nod of acknowledgment.

She must have realised he had no clue who she was because when she stopped the bike in front of him, she said, 'Linda Sampson, Doctor. We met yesterday morning at the corner store. I gave you directions to the clinic and sold you a coffee.'

Weak as water and undrinkable coffee. 'Right, yes.'

'It's good to see you're settling in. Turraburra

has the prettiest beach this side of Wilson's Promontory, don't you think?'

He opened his mouth to say he didn't really have a lot of experience with beaches but she kept right on talking. 'The town's got a lot to offer, especially to families. Are you married, Dr Jackson?'

'No.' He banged his sandy shoe against the sea wall harder than necessary, pining for the anonymity of a big city where no one would think to stop and talk to him if he was sitting on the sea wall at the Middle Park beach.

His life had been put on hold once already and he had no intention of tying himself down to another human being, animal or fish. 'I'm happily single.' If he'd hoped that by telling her that it would get the woman to back off, he was mistaken.

'There's a fine line between happily single and happily coupled up,' Linda said with the enthusiastic smile of a matchmaker. 'And you're in luck. There are some lovely young women in town. The radiographer, Heather Barton, is single.'

One of the other women called out, 'Actually, she's dating Emma Trewella now.'

'Is she? Well, that explains a lot,' Linda said with a laugh. 'Still, that leaves the physiotherapist. She's a gorgeous girl and very into her triathlons. Do you like sports, Doctor?'

He stared at her slack-jawed. Had he been catapulted backwards in time to 1950? He couldn't believe this woman was trying to set him up with someone.

'Or perhaps you'd have more in common with the nurses?' Linda continued. 'I'm sure three of them aren't dating anyone at the moment…'

The memory of ringless white hands gripping pink folders and sky-blue eyes sparking silver arcs shot unbidden into his mind.

'Lucy, Penny and…' Linda paused, turning towards her group. 'What's the name of the pretty nurse with the blonde hair?'

Lilia. He tied his shoe laces with a jerk and reminded himself that he wasn't looking to date anyone and even if he had been, he most certainly wasn't going to date her. Despite her angelic good looks, her personality was at the opposite end of the spectrum. He wouldn't be surprised if she had horns and carried a pitchfork.

'Grace,' someone said. 'Although is she truly blonde?'

Noah stood up quickly, dusting his black pants free of sand. 'That's quite an extensive list, Linda, but I think you've forgotten someone.'

She shook her head, the magpie deterrent cable ties on her helmet swinging wildly. 'I don't think I have.'

'What about the midwife?'

He thought he heard a collective intake of breath from the other women and Linda's smile faltered. 'Lily's married to her job, Doctor. You're much better off dating one of the others.'

The words came with an undercurrent of a warning not to go there. Before he could ask her why, there was a flurry of ringing bike bells, called farewells and the group took off along the path—a bright slash of iridescent yellow wobbling and weaving towards the noon sun.

* * *

Lily stared at the appointment sheet and groaned. How could she have forgotten the date? It was the midwifery centre's bi-monthly doctor clinic. Why had the planets aligned to make it this month? Why not next month when Noah Jackson would be long gone and far, far away? The luck of the Irish or any other nationality was clearly not running her way today. She was going to have to work in close proximity with him all afternoon. Just fantastic...not!

As the town's midwife, Lily operated independently under the auspices of the Melbourne Midwifery Unit. When a newly pregnant woman made contact with her, she conducted a preliminary interview and examination. Some women, due to pre-existing medical conditions such as diabetes or a multiple pregnancy, she immediately referred to the obstetricians at the Victoria or to the Dandenong District Hospital but most women fitted the criteria to be under her care.

However, it wasn't her decision alone. Like the

other independent midwife-run birth units it was modelled on, all pregnant Turraburra clients had to be examined by a doctor once in early pregnancy. Lily scheduled these appointments to take place with the GP on one afternoon every two months. Today was the day.

Her computer beeped with an instant message from Karen.

Grumpy guts is on his way. Good luck! I've put Tim Tams in the kitchen. You'll need three after working with him all afternoon.

Karen had been having a whinge in the tearoom earlier in the day about Dr Jackson. She'd called him cold, curt and a control freak. Lily was used to Karen getting defensive with new staff members who questioned her but she couldn't believe Noah Jackson could be quite as bad as Karen made out. She'd offered Karen chocolate and wisely kept her own counsel.

'You ready?'

The gruff tone had her swinging around on

her office chair. Noah stood in the doorway with his sleeves rolled up to his elbows and one hand pressed up against the doorjamb—muscles bunched and veins bulging. A flicker of something momentarily stirred low in her belly—something she hadn't experienced in a very long time. Fear immediately clenched her muscles against it, trying to force it away. For her own safety she'd locked down her sexual response three years ago and it had to stay that way.

Unlike yesterday, when Noah had looked like the quintessential urban professional, today he was rumpled. His thick hair was wildly wind-ruffled, his tie was stuffed in between the third and fourth buttons of his business shirt and his black trousers bore traces of sand. Had he spent his lunch break at the beach? She loved the calming effects of the ocean and often took ten minutes to regroup between clinic sessions. Perhaps he wasn't as stuck up as she'd first thought. 'Been enjoying the beach?'

Shadows crossed his rich chocolate eyes. 'I wouldn't go so far as to say that.'

She tried hard not to roll her eyes. Perish the thought he might actually find something positive about Turraburra. *Stick to talking about work.* 'Today's clinic is all about—'

'Pregnant women. Yeah, I get it. You do the obs, test their urine and weigh them and leave the rest to me.'

I don't think so. She stood up because sitting with him staring down at her from those arcane eyes she felt way too vulnerable. Three years ago she'd made a commitment to herself that she was never again going to leave herself open to be placed in a powerless position with another human being. Even in low heels she was closer to his height.

'These women are my patients and this is a rubber-stamping exercise so they can be part of the midwifery programme.'

His nostrils flared. 'As the *doctor*, isn't it my decision?'

Spare me from non-team-players. 'I'm sorry, I thought you were a surgical registrar but suddenly you're moonlighting as an obstetrician?'

His cheekbones sharpened as he sucked in a breath through his teeth and she reeled in her fraying temper. What was it about this man that made her break her own rules of never reacting? Of never provoking a man to anger? Of never putting herself at risk? She also didn't want to give Noah Jackson any excuse to dismiss her as *that crazy midwife* and interfere with her programme.

'I take that back. As Turraburra's midwife, with five years' experience, anyone I feel doesn't qualify for the programme has already been referred on.'

His gaze hooked hers, brimming with discontent. 'So, in essence, this clinic is a waste of my time?'

'It's protocol.'

'Fine.' He spun on his heel, crossed the hall and disappeared into the examination room.

She sighed and hurried in after him.

'Bec,' she said to the pregnant woman who was sitting, waiting, 'this is Dr Jackson, our current locum GP. As I explained, he'll be examining you today.'

Bec Sinclair, a happy-go-lucky woman, gave an expansive smile. 'No worries. Good to meet you, Doc.'

Noah sat down behind the desk and gave her a brisk nod before turning his attention to the computer screen and reading her medical history. He frowned. 'You had a baby eight months ago and you're pregnant again?'

Bec laughed at his blatant disapproval. 'It was a bit of a surprise, that's for sure.'

'I gather you weren't organised enough to use contraception.'

Lily's jaw dropped open. She couldn't believe he'd just said that.

Bec, to her credit, didn't seem at all fazed by his rudeness. 'It was a dodgy condom but no harm done. We wanted another baby so the fact it's coming a year earlier than planned is no biggie.' She leaned towards the desk, showing Noah a photo of her little boy on her phone. 'Lily delivered Harley, and Jase and I really want her to deliver this next one too.'

'It will be my pleasure. Harley's really cute, isn't he, Noah?' Lily said, giving him an opening for some chitchat and hoping he'd respond.

Noah ignored her and the proffered photo. Instead, he pushed back from the desk, stood and pulled the curtain around the examination table. Patting it with his hand, he said, 'Up you get.'

Bec exchanged a look with Lily that said *Is this guy for real?* before rising and climbing up the three small steps.

Lily made her comfortable and positioned the modesty sheet before returning to stand by Bec's head. Noah silently listened to her heart, examined her breasts and then her abdomen. Lily kept up a patter, explaining to Bec everything that Noah was doing because, apparently, he'd turned mute.

When the examination was over and Bec was back in the chair, Noah said, 'Everything seems fine, except that you're fat.'

Bec paled.

'What Dr Jackson means,' Lily said hurriedly, as she threw at him what she hoped was a venomous look, 'is that you're still carrying some weight from your last pregnancy.'

'That's not what I meant at all.' Noah pulled up a BMI chart, spun the computer screen towards Bec and pointed to the yellow overweight zone where it met the red obese one. 'Right now, you're just below the border of obese. If you're not careful during this pregnancy, you'll tip into the red zone. That will put you at risk of complications such as gestational diabetes, pre-eclampsia and thrombosis. There's also an increased risk that the baby may end up being in a difficult position such as breech. All of those things would make you ineligible to be delivered by Lilia at the birth centre.'

'I want to have my baby here,' Bec said, her voice suddenly wobbly.

'Then make sure you exercise and eat healthy foods. It's that simple.' Noah turned to Lily. 'I assume you have information for your patients about that sort of thing.'

'I do,' she managed to grind out between clenched teeth. 'If you come with me, Bec, I'll give the pamphlets to you now as well as the water aerobics timetable. It's a fun way to exercise and there's a crèche at the pool.'

She escorted Bec from the room and gave her all the information, along with small packet of tissues. 'Come and see me tomorrow and we'll talk about it all then in greater detail. Okay?'

Bec nodded and sniffed. 'I kinda knew I'd got big but it was hard hearing it.'

Lily could have killed Noah. 'I'm so sorry.'

'Don't be. It's not your fault.' Bec gave a long sigh. 'I guess I needed to hear it.'

She gave Bec's shoulder a squeeze. 'Only in a kinder way.'

'Yeah.' Bec took in a deep breath. 'I didn't know being heavy could make things dangerous for me and the baby, and I guess it's good that he told me because I don't want to have to go to Melbourne. I know Mandy Carmichael's preggers again and she's pretty big. Maybe we can help each other, you know?'

Lily smiled encouragingly. 'That sounds like a great plan.'

As Bec left, Karen buzzed her. 'Kat Nguyen's rescheduled for later today so you've got a gap.'

As Lily hung up the phone she knew exactly what she was going to do with her free half-hour, whether she wanted to take that risk or not.

Noah glanced up as Lily walked back into the office alone. Her face was tight with tension and disapproving lines bracketed her mouth, pulling it down at the edges. An irrational desire to see her smile tugged at him and that on its own annoyed him. So what if a smile made her eyes crinkle at the edges with laughter lines and caused dimples to score her cheeks? So what if a smile made her light up, look happy and full of life and chased away her usual closed-off sangfroid? Made her look pretty?

He tried to shake off the feeling. It was nothing to him whether she was happy or not. Whether she was a workaholic or not, like the ladies at the beach had told him. Whether she was anything other than the pain in the rear that she'd already proved to be. He didn't have time in his life for a woman who was fun, let alone one with dragon tendencies. 'Where's the next patient?'

She crossed her arms. 'She's running late.'

He'd already pegged her as a person who liked things to go her own way and a late patient would throw out her schedule. 'So that's why you're looking like you've just sucked on a lemon. Surely you know nothing in the medical profession ever runs on time.'

Her eyes rounded and widened so far he could have tumbled into their pale, azure depths. 'Are you stressed or ill?'

'No,' he said, seriously puzzled. 'Why would you say that?'

She walked closer to the desk. 'So you're just naturally rude.'

Baffled by her accusations, he held onto his temper by the barest of margins. That surprised him. Usually he'd have roared like a lion if a nurse or anyone more junior to him had dared to speak to him like this. 'Where's all this antagonism coming from? Did something happen to upset you while you were out of the room?'

'Where's all this coming from?' Incredulity pushed her voice up from its usual throaty depths. 'You just told Bec Sinclair she's fat.'

He didn't get why she was all het up. 'So? I said that because she is.'

She pressed her palms down on the desk and as she leaned in he caught the light scent of spring flowers and something else he couldn't name. 'Yes, but you didn't have to tell her quite so baldly. Do you ever think before you speak?'

Her accusation had him shooting to his feet to rectify the power balance. 'Of course I do. She needed to know the risks that her weight adds to her pregnancy. I told her the truth.'

Her light brown brows hit her hairline. 'You're brutally blunt.'

'No. I'm honest with them.'

She shook her head back and forth so fast he thought she'd give herself whiplash. 'Oh, no, you're not getting away with that. There are ways of telling someone the truth and you're using it as an excuse to be thoughtless and rude.'

She'd just crossed the line in the sand he'd already moved for her. 'Look, Miss Manners,' he said tersely. 'You don't have the right to storm in here and accuse me of being rude.'

Her shoulders rolled back like an Amazon woman preparing for battle. 'I do when it affects *my* patients. You just reduced the most laid-back, easygoing woman I know to tears.'

A pang of conscience jabbed him. Had he really done that? 'She was upset?'

She threw her hands up. 'You think? Yes, of course she was upset.'

He rubbed his hand over the back of his neck as he absorbed that bit of information. 'I didn't realise I'd upset her.'

Lily dropped into the chair, her expression stunned. 'You're kidding me, right?'

No. Man, he hated general practice with its touchy-feely stuff and rules that he hadn't known existed. He was a surgeon and a damn good one. He diagnosed problems and then he cut them out.

As a result, he gave people a better quality of life. It was a far easier way of dealing with problems than the muddy waters of internal medicine where nothing was cut and dried and everything was hazy with irrational hope.

He and his mother had learned that the hard way and after that life-changing experience he'd vowed he would always give his patients the truth. Black was black and white was white. People needed information so they could make a choice.

The prof's voice came out of nowhere, echoing loudly in his head. *We've had complaints from your dealings with patients when they're awake.*

His legs trembled and he sat down hard, nausea churning his gut. Was this the sort of thing the prof had been referring to? Propping his elbows on the desk, he ran his hands through his hair and tried to marshal his thoughts. Did Lilia actually have a point? Was his interpretation of the facts blunt and thoughtless?

He instantly railed against the idea, refusing to believe it for a moment. *We've had complaints.*

The prof's words were irrefutable. As much as he didn't want to acknowledge it, *this* was the reason he'd been sent down here to Turraburra. It seemed he really did have a problem communicating with patients. A problem he hadn't been fully aware of until this moment. A problem that was going to stop him from qualifying as a surgeon if he didn't do something about it.

'Noah?'

There was no trace of the previous anger in her voice and none of the sarcasm. All he could hear was concern. He raised his eyes to hers, his gaze stalling on the lushness of her lips. Pink and moist, they were slightly parted. Kissable. Oh, so very kissable. What they would taste like? Icy cool, like her usual demeanour, or sizzling hot, like she'd been a moment ago when she'd taken him to task? Or sweet and decadently rich? Perhaps sharply tart with a kick of fire?

The tip of her tongue suddenly darted out, flicking the peak of her top lip before falling back. Heat slammed into him, rushing lust through him and down into every cell as if he were an inexperienced teen. Hell, he had more control than this. He sucked in a breath and gave thanks he was sitting down behind a desk, his lap hidden from view.

He shifted his gaze to the safety of her nose, which, although it suited her face, wasn't cute or sexy. This brought his traitorous body back under control. He didn't want to be attracted to Lilia Cartwright in any shape or form. He just wanted to get this time in Turraburra over and done with and get the hell out of town. Get back to the security of the Melbourne Victoria and to the job he loved above all else.

Her previously flinty gaze was now soft and caring. 'Noah, is everything okay?'

Everything's so far from okay it's not funny. Could he tell her the real reason the Victoria had sent a surgeon to Turraburra? Tell her that if he didn't conquer this communication problem he wouldn't qualify? That ten years of hard work had failed to give him what he so badly wanted?

For the first time since he'd met her he saw genuine interest and empathy in her face and a part of him desperately wanted to reach out and confide in her. God knew, if he'd unwittingly upset a patient and been clueless about the impact of his words, he surely needed help.

She'll understand.

You don't know that. She could just as easily use it against me.

He'd fought long and hard to get this far in the competitive field of surgery without depending on anyone and he didn't intend to start now. That said, he'd noticed how relaxed she was with her patients compared to how he always felt with them. With Bec Sinclair, she'd explained everything he'd been doing, chatting easily to her. She connected with people in a way he'd never been able to—in a way he needed to learn.

He had no intention of asking her for help or exposing any weakness, but that didn't mean he couldn't observe and learn from her. *Don't give anything away.* Leaning back, he casually laced his fingers behind his head. 'Do you have any other fat pregnant women coming in today?'

Wariness crawled across her high cheekbones. 'There is one more.'

'Do you concede that her weight is a risk to her pregnancy?'

'Yes, but—'

'Good.' He sat forward fast, the chair clunking loudly. 'This time you run the consultation, which means you're the one who has to tell her that her weight is a problem.'

She blinked at him in surprise and then her intelligent eyes narrowed, scanning his face like an explosives expert looking for undetonated bombs. 'And?'

'And then I'll critique your performance like you just critiqued mine. After all, the Victoria's a teaching hospital so it seems only fair.'

He couldn't help but grin at her stunned expression.

CHAPTER THREE

LILY TURNED THE music up and sang loudly as she drove through the rolling hills and back towards the coast and Turraburra. As well as singing, she concentrated on the view. Anything to try and still her mind and stop it from darting to places she didn't want it to go.

She savoured the vista of black and white cows dotted against the emerald-green paddocks—the vibrant colour courtesy of spring rains. Come January, the grass would be scorched brown and the only green would be the feathery tops of the beautiful white-barked gumtrees.

She'd been out at the Hawkers' dairy farm, doing a follow-up postnatal visit. Jess and the baby were both doing well and Richard had baked scones, insisting she stay for morning tea. She'd found it hard to believe that the burly farmer was capable of knocking out a batch of scones, because the few men who'd passed through her life hadn't been cooks. When she'd confessed her surprise to Richard, he'd just laughed and said, 'If I depended on Jess to cook, we'd both have starved years ago.'

'I have other talents,' Jess, the town's lawyer, said without rancour.

'That you do,' Richard had replied with such a look of love and devotion in his eyes that it had made Lily's throat tighten.

She'd grown up hearing the stories from her grandfather of her parents' love for each other but she had no memory of it. Somehow it had always seemed like a story just out of reach—like a fairy-tale and not at all real. Sure, she had their wedding photo framed on her dresser but plenty of people got married and it ended in recriminations and pain. She was no stranger to that scenario and she often wondered if her parents had lived longer lives, they would still be together.

Although her grandfather loved her dearly,

she'd never known the sort of love that Jess and Richard shared. She'd hoped for it when she'd met Trent and had allowed herself to be seduced by the idea of it. She'd learned that when a fairy-tale met reality, the fallout was bitter and life-changing. As a result, and for her own protection, and in a way for the protection of her mythical child, she wasn't prepared to risk another relationship. The only times she questioned her decision was when she saw true love in action, like today.

Her loud, off-key singing wasn't banishing her unsettling thoughts like it usually did. Ever since Noah Jackson had burst into Turraburra—all stormy-eyed and difficult—troubling thoughts had become part of her again. She couldn't work him out. She wanted to say he was rude, arrogant, self-righteous and exasperating, and dismiss him out of her head. He was definitely all of those things but then there were moments when he looked so adrift—like yesterday when he'd appeared genuinely stunned and upset that his words had distressed Bec Sinclair. She couldn't work him out.

You don't have to work him out. You don't have to work any man out. Remember, it's safer not to even try.

Except that momentary look of bewilderment on his face had broken through his *I'm a surgeon, bow down before me* facade, and it had got to her. It had humanised him and she wished it hadn't. Arrogant Noah was far more easily dismissed as a temporary thorn in her side than thoughtful Noah. The Noah who'd sat back and listened intently and watched without a hint of disparagement as she'd talked with Mandy Carmichael about her weight was an intriguing conundrum.

She braked at the four-way intersection and proceeded to turn right, passing the *Welcome to Turraburra* sign. She smiled at the '+1' someone had painted next to the population figure. Given the number of pregnant women in town at the moment, she expected to see a lot more graffiti over the coming months. Checking the clock on the dash, she decided that she had just enough time to check in on her grandfather before starting afternoon clinic.

Her phone beeped as it always did when she drove back into town after being in a mobile phone reception dead zone. This time, instead of one or two messages, it vibrated wildly as six messages came in one after another. She immediately pulled over.

11:00 Unknown patient in labour. Go to hospital.
Karen.

11:15 Visitor to town in established labour in Emergency. Your assistance appreciated.
N. Jackson.

'What have you done with the Noah Jackson I know and despair of?' she said out loud. The formal style of Noah's text was unexpected and it made Karen's seem almost brusque in comparison. The juxtaposition made her smile.

11:50 Contractions now two minutes apart. Last baby I delivered was six years ago. Request immediate assistance.
NJ.

12:10 Where the bloody hell are you?!
N.

'And he's back.' Although, to give Noah his due, she'd be totally stressed out if she was being asked to do something she hadn't done in a very long time. She threw the car into gear, checked over her shoulder and pulled off the gravel. Three minutes later she was running into Emergency to the familiar groans of a woman in transition.

For the first time since arriving in Turraburra, Noah was genuinely happy to see starchy and standoffish Lilia Cartwright, Midwife. 'You don't text, you don't call,' he tried to joke against a taut throat. Trying to stop himself from yelling, *I'm freaking out here and where the hell have you been?*

'Sorry,' she said breezily. 'I was out of range.'

'Seriously?' Her statement stunned him. 'You don't have mobile reception when you leave town? That's not safe for your patients. What if a woman delivers when you're not here?'

'Welcome to the country, Noah. We'd love to have the communications coverage that you get in the city but the infrastructure isn't here.'

'How can people live like this?' he muttered, adding yet another reason to his long list of why country life sucked.

'I always let Karen know where I am and a message gets to me eventually.'

'Oh, and that's so very reassuring.'

She rolled her eyes. 'I'm here now so you can stop panicking.'

Indignation rolled through him. 'I. Do. Not. Panic.'

'I'm sure you don't when you're in your beloved operating theatre, but this isn't your area of expertise and it's normal to be nervous when you're out of your comfort zone.'

Her expression was devoid of any judgement.

In fact, all he could read on her face was understanding and that confused him. Made him suspicious. If surgery had taught him anything it was that life was a competition. Any sign of weakness would and could be used to further someone else's career. He'd expected her to take this as another opportunity to show him up. Highlight his failings, as she'd done so succinctly yesterday. He'd never expected her to be empathetic.

As she pulled on a disposable plastic apron she flicked her braid to one side, exposing her long, creamy neck. He was suddenly engulfed by the scent of apples, cherries and mangoes, which took him straight back to the memories of long-past summers growing up and fruit salad and ice cream.

Regret that midwives no longer wore gowns slugged him hard. Back in the day he would have needed to tie her gown and his fingers would have brushed against that warm, smooth skin. His heart kicked up at the thought, pumping heat through him.

What are you doing? She's so not your type and you don't even like her.

That was true on all fronts. He limited his dating to women who were fun, flirty and only interested in a good time. A good time that ended the moment they planned beyond two weeks in advance. Somehow he got the feeling that Lilia wasn't that type of woman.

With the apron tied, she lifted her head and caught him staring at her. Her fingers immediately brushed her cheeks. 'What? Do I have jam or cream on my mouth from morning tea?'

'No.' Embarrassment made the word sound curt and sharp and she tensed. He instantly regretted his tone and sighed. 'Sorry. Can I please tell you about your patient?'

'Yes.' She sounded as relieved as him. 'Fill me in.'

Happy to be back in familiar territory, he commenced a detailed patient history. 'Jade Riccardo, primigravida, thirty-seven weeks pregnant. She's been visiting relatives in town and arrived here an hour ago in established labour. Foetal heart rate's strong and, going on my rusty palpation skills, the baby's in an anterior position. Her husband's with her but they're both understandably anxious because they're booked in to have the baby in Melbourne.'

A long, loud groan came from the other side of the door. 'Sounds like she's going to have it in Turraburra and very soon.' Lilia grinned up at him, her dimples diving deep into her cheeks and her eyes as bright as a summer's day. She was full of enthusiastic anticipation while he was filled with dread. She tugged on his arm. 'Come on, then. Let's go deliver a baby.'

The heat of her hand warmed him and he missed it when she pulled it away. He followed her into the room and introduced her. 'Jade, Paul, this is Lilia Cartwright, Turraburra's midwife.'

Jade, who was fully in the transition zone, didn't respond. She was on all fours, rocking back and forth and sucking on nitrous oxide like it was oxygen.

Paul was rubbing Jade's back and he threw a

grateful look to both of them. 'Are you sure everything's okay? She's doing a lot of grunting.'

Lilia smiled. 'That's great. It means she's working with her body and getting ready to push the baby out.' She rested her hand on Jade's shoulder. 'Hi, Jade. I know this is all moving faster than you expected and it's not happening where you expected, but lots of babies have been born in Turraburra, haven't they, Noah?'

'Yes.'

She rolled her eyes.

Beads of sweat pooled on Noah's brow. Her resigned look spoke volumes, telling him he was failing at something. He looked at the husband, whose face was tight with worry. 'Lots of babies,' he echoed Lilia, practising how to be reassuring and hoping he could pull it off. 'It might not be Melbourne but you're in good hands.' *Lilia's hands.*

Paul visibly relaxed. 'That's good to know.'

Lilia placed one hand on Jade's abdomen and her other on her buttocks. 'With the next contraction, Jade, I want you to push down here.'

Jade groaned.

'Your tummy's tightening. I can feel one coming now.'

Jade sucked on the nitrous oxide and then pushed, making a low guttural sound.

Lilia pulled on gloves. 'You're doing great, Jade. I can see some black hair.'

Paul stroked Jade's hair, his face excited. 'Did you hear that, honey?'

Contraction over, Jade slumped down onto the pillows. 'I can't do this.'

'You're already doing it, Jade,' Lilia said calmly. 'Every contraction takes you closer to holding your baby in your arms.'

Noah, feeling as useless as a bike without wheels, did what he knew best—busied himself with the surgical instruments. He snapped on gloves, unwrapped the sterilised delivery pack, set out the bowl, the forceps and scissors, and added the cord clamps, all the while listening to Lilia's soothing voice giving instructions and praising Jade.

They developed a rhythm, with Paul encouraging Jade, Lilia focusing on the baby's descent and Noah checking the baby's heartbeat after each contraction. Each time the rushing sound of horses' hooves sounded, Paul would grin at him and he found himself smiling back. With each contraction, the baby's head moved down a little further until twenty minutes later it sat bulging on the perineum, ready to be born.

'I think you're going to have your baby with the next contraction,' Lilia said as her fingers controlled the baby's head. 'Pant, Jade, pant.'

Jade tried to pant and then groaned. 'Can't.' With a loud grunt, she pushed. A gush of fluid heralded the baby's head, which appeared a moment later, its face scrunched and surprised.

'The baby's head is born. Well done,' Lilia said.

'Our baby's nearly here, honey,' Paul's voice cracked with emotion. 'I can see the head.

'I want it to stop,' Jade sobbed. 'It's too hard.'

Noah looked at the sweaty and exhausted woman who'd endured an incredibly fast and intense labour. She was so very close to finishing and he recalled how once he'd almost stopped running in a marathon because his body had felt like it had been melting in pain. A volunteer had called out to him, 'You've done the hard yards, mate, keep going, the prize is in sight.' It was exactly what he'd needed to hear and it had carried him home.

'The hard work's over, Jade,' he said quietly. 'You can do this. One more push.' He caught Lilia's combined look of surprise and approval streak across her face and he had a ridiculous urge to high-five someone.

Jade's hand shot out and gripped Noah's shoulder, her wild eyes fixed on his. 'Promise?'

'Promise.'

'Noah's right, Jade,' Lilia confirmed. 'With the next contraction, I'll deliver the baby's shoulders and the rest of him or her will follow.'

'Okay. I can feel a contraction *noooooow*.' Jade pushed.

A dusky baby slithered into Lilia's arms and something deep down inside Noah moved. It had been years since he'd been present at a birth and he'd forgotten how amazing it was to witness the arrival of new life into the world.

Lilia clamped the umbilical cord before asking the stunned father, 'Do you want to cut the cord, Paul?'

'Yes.' With shaking hands, Paul cut where Lilia indicated and then said, with wonder in his voice, 'It's a little girl, Jade.'

Noah rubbed the baby with a towel and took note of her breathing and colour and muscle tone so he could give an Apgar score for the first minute of life. The baby hadn't cried but her dark eyes were bright and gazing around, taking in this new world. A lump formed in his throat and he immediately tried to get rid of it because emotion opened a guy up to being weak and vulnerable.

'I'm going to pass the baby between your legs, Jade,' Lilia said. 'Are you ready?'

'My arms are shaking and I'm getting another contraction.'

Paul took the baby, cradling her in his arms while Lilia delivered the placenta. As she examined it, Noah helped Jade roll over. 'In an hour we can transfer you to the midwifery unit. You'll be a lot more comfortable there.'

Paul reverently passed his daughter to his wife. 'Meet Jasmine.'

Silent tears rolled down Jade's cheeks as she unwrapped the baby and counted her fingers and toes. 'Hey, sweetie, I'm your mummy.'

Noah stepped back, moving to the corner of the room and standing next to Lilia, who was breathing deeply. He glanced at her. Her beautiful blue eyes shone with unshed tears but her face was wreathed in a smile. She was luminous with joy and it radiated from her like white light.

With a jolt, he realised this was the first time he'd ever seen her look truly happy. It called out to him so strongly that his body leaned in of its own accord until his head was close to hers and her fresh, fruity perfume filled his nostrils. He wanted to wrap his arms around her, kiss her long and slow and harvest her jubilation. Keep it safe.

Get a grip. You're at work and this is Lilia,

remember? The ice queen and dragon rolled into one.

Shocked at what he'd almost done, he covered by saying quietly so only she could hear, 'You did an amazing job. It was very impressive.' The words came out rough and gruff and he jerked his head back, putting much-needed distance between them.

'Thanks.' She blew her nose. 'Sorry. I'm a bit of a sook and it gets to me every time.'

He took in the new family—their love and awe swirling around them in a life-affirming way. It both warmed and scared him. 'I guess I can understand that.'

She tilted her head and gave him a long, considering look. 'I'm glad. You did okay yourself.'

In his world, okay didn't come close to being good enough. 'Just okay?'

She laughed. 'Fishing for compliments, Noah?'

He found himself smiling at her directness. 'I might be.'

'Then let me put it this way. You did better today than you did yesterday.'

That didn't tell him very much at all. 'And?'

'And empathy doesn't come easily to you.'

She walked back to the bed to do a mother and baby check and he let his gaze drop to admire the swing of her hips. Part of him hated that she'd worked out he struggled to be naturally sympathetic and another part of him was glad. All of it added together discombobulated him, especially his response to her. How could he be driven to madness by her one minute and want to kiss her senseless the next?

Suddenly surviving four weeks in Turraburra just got harder for a whole different set of reasons.

Two days later Lilia waved goodbye to the Riccardos, who were keen to get back to Melbourne with Jasmine. She'd arranged for the district nurse to visit them so they'd have help when Jade's milk came in and to cover the days before the maternal and child health nurse visited. As she closed off the file, an unusual wistfulness filled her. She was used to farewelling couples but usually she knew she'd see them again around town and she'd be able to watch the baby grow. She hoped the Riccardos would call in the next time they were in town and visiting relatives, so she could get her little Jasmine fix. She really was a cute baby.

Lily had been beyond surprised when Noah had called in first thing this morning, insisting on doing a discharge check. She'd assumed he'd handed Jade and Jasmine's care over to her the moment she'd stepped into Emergency and he'd said, 'Can I tell you about *your* patient?' Even though she'd seen him try really hard to connect with Jade and Paul during the fast labour, she'd thought he probably much preferred to be far away from such patient intimacy.

Apparently, she'd been wrong.

He'd spent ten minutes with the Riccardos but in reality it had been way more of a cuddle of Jasmine than a discharge check. Always taut with tension, as if he needed to be alert and ready for anything, Noah had seemed almost relaxed as he'd cradled the swaddled baby—well, relaxed for him anyway. She'd been transfixed by the image of the tiny newborn snuggled up against his broad chest and held safely in his strong arms—his sun-kissed skin a honey brown against the white baby shawl.

The idea of arms providing shelter instead of harm burrowed into her mind and tried to set up residence. For a tempting moment she allowed it to. She even let herself feel and enjoy the tingling warmth spinning through her at the thought of Noah's arms wrapped around her, before she rejected all of it firmly and irrevocably. Entertaining ideas like that only led her down a dangerous path—one she'd vowed never to hike along again. It was one thing for other people to take a risk on a relationship but after what had happened with Trent she wasn't ever trusting her judgement with men again.

At almost the same time as she'd locked down her wayward body and thoughts Noah had quickly handed the baby back to Jade, stood abruptly, and with a brisk and brief goodbye had left the room. Paul had commented in a puzzled voice, 'I guess he needs to see a patient.'

Lily, who'd been busy getting her own emotions back under control, had suspected Noah had experienced a rush of affection for the baby and hadn't known how to process it. Like her, he probably had his reasons for avoiding feeling too much of anything and running from it when it caught him unawares.

Time to stop thinking about Noah Jackson.

Shaking her shoulders to slough off the unwanted thoughts, she set about preparing for her new mothers' group that was meeting straight after lunch. She was talking to them, amongst other things, about immunisation. Too many people took for granted the good health that life in Australia afforded them and didn't understand that whooping cough could still kill a young child.

'Ah, Lily?'

She glanced up to see Karen standing in the doorway. Karen rarely walked all the way back here to the annexe, preferring instead to use the intercom. The medical secretary ran the practice her way and she liked to have all the 'i's dotted and the 't's crossed.

Lily racked her brain to think if she'd forgotten some vital piece of paperwork but came up blank. 'Hi, Karen. Whatever I did wrong, I'm sorry,' she said with a laugh. 'Tell me how to fix it.'

Karen shook her head. 'It's not about work, Lily. The hospital just called and your grandfather's in Emergency.'

Gramps! No. Her hand gripped the edge of her desk as a thousand terrifying thoughts closed in on her. At eighty-five, any number of things could have happened to him—stroke, heart attack, a fall. She didn't want to consider any of them.

Karen shoved Lily's handbag into her arms and pushed her towards the door. 'You go to the hospital and don't worry about work. I'll call all the new mums and cancel this afternoon's session.'

'Thanks, Karen, you're the best.' She was already out the door and running down the disabled entry ramp. She crossed the courtyard gardens and entered the emergency department via the back entrance, all the while frantically praying that Gramps was going to be okay.

Panting, she stopped at the desk. 'Where is he?'

'Room one,' Bronwyn Patterson, the emergency nurse manager, said kindly, and pointed the direction.

'Thanks.' Not stopping to chat, she tugged open the door of the resus room and almost fell through the doorway. Her grandfather lay on a narrow trolley propped up on pillows and looking as pale as the sheet that covered him. 'Gramps? What happened?'

He took in her heaving chest and what was probably a panicked look on her face and raised his thin, bony arm. 'Calm down, Lily. I'm fine.'

She caught a flicker of movement in the corner of her eye and realised Noah was in the room. He raised his head from studying an ECG tracing and his thoughtful gaze sought hers.

'Hello, Lilia.'

There was a slight trace of censuring amusement in his tone that she'd just barged into the room and completely ignored him. She knew if he'd done that to her, she'd have been critical of him. 'Hello, Noah. How's my grandfather?'

'He fainted.'

The succinct words made her swing her attention back to her grandfather. 'Did you eat breakfast?' Her fear and concern came out as interrogation.

'Of course I ate my breakfast and I had morning tea,' he said grumpily, responding to her tone. 'When have you ever known me to be off my tucker? And before you ask, I took all my tablets too. I just stood up too quickly at exercise class.'

You're lucky you didn't break a hip. She noticed a wad of gauze taped to his arm and a telltale red stain in the centre. 'What happened to your arm?'

'Just a superficial cut. Don't get all het up.' He wriggled up the pillows and glared at her in a very un-Gramps way. 'Isn't there a baby you need to go and deliver?'

She sat down hard on the chair next to him, pressing her handbag into her thighs. 'I'm not going anywhere until I know you're okay.'

'Fine, but don't fuss.' Her usually easygoing grandfather crossed his arms and pouted.

'Let me know when both of you want my opinion,' Noah said drily.

Her grandfather laughed, his bad mood fading. 'You didn't tell me this one's got a sense of humour, Lily.'

I didn't know he did. She wanted to deny she'd ever spoken about Noah at home but there'd be no point given it was obvious she'd discussed him with her grandfather. Embarrassment raced through her and she could feel the heat on her face and knew she was blushing bright pink.

Noah shot her a challenging look. 'I'm not sure your granddaughter would agree with your assessment of my sense of humour, Mr Cartwright.'

'Call me Bruce, Doc. Now, why did I faint?'

'Your heart rate's very slow.'

'That's good, isn't it? Means I'm fit for my age?'

Lily put her hand on Gramps's and waited for Noah to explain. She hoped he was able to do it using words her grandfather could understand and do it without scaring him.

Noah held up the tracing strip. 'The ECG tells me there's a block in the electrical circuitry of your heart, in the part that controls how fast it beats. When the message doesn't get through, your heart beats too slowly and not enough blood is pumped out. That makes you faint.'

Bruce looked thoughtful. 'Sounds like I need some rewiring.'

This time Noah laughed. 'More like a new starter motor but, yes, some wires are involved. It's called a pacemaker and it's a small procedure done by an electrophysiologist at a day-stay cardiac unit. I can refer you to the pacemaker clinic in Melbourne.'

'Is there anywhere closer?' Bruce asked.

Lily expected Noah to give his usual grunt of annoyance that a country person would want to use a country hospital.

Noah rubbed the back of his neck. 'There's a clinic at Dandenong, which is closer to Turraburra. I could refer you there if you don't want to go all the way to the centre of the city.'

She blinked. Was this the same doctor from the start of the week?

'Well, that all sounds reasonable,' Bruce said, squeezing her hand. 'What do you think, Lily? It will be easier for you if I don't go to Melbourne, won't it?'

Her throat thickened with emotion. Even when her grandfather was sick, he was still putting her first. 'It's your choice, Gramps.'

'Dandenong it is, then.'

'Can I get you anything?' she asked, wanting to focus on practical things rather than the surging relief that she wouldn't have to take him to Melbourne.

'A cup of tea and some sandwiches would be lovely, sweetpea.'

She felt Noah's gaze on her and a tingle of awareness whooshed across her skin. Looking up, she found his dark, inscrutable eyes studying her in the same intense way she'd noticed on other occasions. As usual, with him, she couldn't tell if it was a critical or a complimentary gaze, but its effect made her feel hot and cold, excited and apprehensive, and it left her jittery. She didn't like jittery. It reminded her far too much of the early days with Trent when lust had drained her brain of all common sense. She wasn't allowing that to happen ever again.

'Is it okay for Gramps to have some food?'

Noah seemed to snap out of his trance. 'Sure, if you can call what the kitchen here serves up food,' he said abruptly. He scrawled an order on the chart and left the room.

'See what I have to put up with, Gramps?' she said, feeling baffled that Noah could go from reasonable to rude in a heartbeat.

'He seems like an okay bloke to me. Now, go get me those sandwiches and some cake. A man could starve to death here.'

CHAPTER FOUR

NOAH FOUND LILY sitting in the staff tearoom in the emergency department. *Her name is Lilia*, he reminded himself sharply.

When his phone had woken him at three that morning with an emergency call, it had pulled him out of a delicious dream where he'd been kissing her long, delectable and creamy neck. He'd woken hard, hot and horrified. Right then he'd vowed he was only ever using her formal and full name. It wasn't as pretty or as soft as Lily and that made it easier to think of her as a one-sided equation—defensive and critical with hard edges. He didn't want to spend any time thinking about the talented midwife, the caring granddaughter and the very attractive woman.

Doing that was fraught with complications given they sparked like jumper leads if they got within a metre of each other. Hell, they had enough electricity running between them to power Bruce Cartwright's heart. Working in Turraburra was complication enough given the closeness of his exams. He wasn't adding chasing a woman who had no qualms speaking her mind, frequently found him lacking and gave no sign he was anything more to her than a doctor she had to put up with for four long weeks.

She intrigues you.

No, she annoys me and I'm not pursuing this. Hell, he didn't pursue women any more, full stop—he didn't have to. Since qualifying as a doctor, women had taken to pursuing him and he picked and chose as he pleased, always making sure he could walk away.

Seriously, can you hear yourself?

Shut up.

Needing coffee, he strode to the coffee-machine and immediately swore softly. The pod container was empty.

'Do you need to attend a meeting for your coffee addiction?' Lilia asked with a hint of a smile on her bee-stung lips as she handed him a teabag.

'Probably.' He filled a mug with boiling water. 'I suppose I should be happy you didn't tell me to put money in a swear jar.'

Her eyes sparkled. 'Oh, now, there's an idea. With you here filling it ten times a day, I could probably go on a cruise at the end of the month.'

He raised his brows at her comment. 'And if I instigated a sarcasm jar, so could I.'

'Touché.' She raised her mug to her mouth and sipped her tea, her brow furrowed in thought. 'Thanks for picking up Gramps's heart block so fast.'

He shrugged, unnerved by this almost conciliatory Lilia. 'It's what I'm paid to do.'

She rolled her eyes. 'And he takes a compliment so well.'

He wasn't touching that. 'Your grandfather's not doing too badly for eighty-five.'

Shadows darkened the sky blue of her eyes. 'He's not doing as well as he has been. I've noticed a definite slowing down recently, which he isn't happy about. As you saw, he's an independent old coot.'

He jiggled his teabag. 'Does he live alone?'

She shook her head. 'No. I live with him.'

He thought about the two long years he'd been tied to home, living and caring for his sick mother. Eight years may have passed since then, but the memories of how he'd constantly lurched between resentment that his life was on hold and guilt that he dared feel that way remained vivid. It still haunted him—the self-reproach, the isolation, the feelings of uselessness, the overwhelming responsibility. 'Doesn't living with your grandfather cramp your style?'

She gave him a bewildered look and then burst into peals of laughter, the sound as joyous as the ringing bells of a carillon. 'I don't have any style to cramp. Besides, I've been living with him since I was four. My parents died fighting the bush fires that razed the district twenty-seven years ago.'

'That must have been tough for you.'

She shrugged. 'I was two when it happened

and, sure, there were times growing up when I wondered if my life might have been different if my parents had lived, but I never lacked for love. Somehow Gramps not only coped with his own grief at losing his son and daughter-in-law but he did a great job raising me.'

She sounded very together for someone who'd lost both parents. 'He's a remarkable man.'

'He is.' She gave a self-deprecating grimace. 'Even more so for not dispatching me off to boarding school when I was fifteen, running wild and being particularly difficult.'

'One of those times you were wondering about what life would have been like if your parents were still alive?'

She tilted her head and her gaze was thoughtful. 'You know, you may be right. I never thought about it that way. All I remember is playing up and testing Gramps.'

He found himself smiling. 'I can't imagine you being difficult.'

Her pretty mouth curved upwards, its expression ironic. 'Perhaps we both need a sarcasm jar.'

Her smile made him want to lean in close so he could feel her breath on his face and inhale her scent. He immediately leaned back, desperate to cool the simmering attraction he couldn't seem to totally shut down, no matter what he did.

Stick to the topic of work. 'The insertion of the pacemaker should be straightforward but, even so, you need to give some thought to what happens if he continues to go downhill.'

Her plump lips pursed as her shoulders straightened. 'There's nothing to think about. He cared for me so I'll care for him.'

He drummed his fingers against the tabletop, remembering his own similarly worded and heartfelt declaration, and the inevitable fallout that had followed because he'd not thought any of it through. His life had become hijacked by good intentions. 'How will you work the unpredictable hours you do and still manage to care for him?'

Her chin tilted up. 'I'll find a way.'

'Really?' Memories of feeling trapped pushed down on him. 'What happens when you're called out to deliver a baby in the middle of the night and Bruce can't be left home alone? What happens when you have a woman in labour for longer than a few hours? You could be gone for two days at a time and what happens then? You haven't fully thought it through.'

Lily watched Noah become increasingly tense and fervent and she couldn't fathom where his vehemence was coming from. Despite his slight improvement with patients, this was a man who generally saw people in terms of disconnected body parts, not as whole people with thoughts and feelings and a place in a family and community. Why was he suddenly stressing about something that didn't remotely concern him.

'I live in a community that cares, Noah. People will help.'

'Good luck with that,' he muttered almost bitterly, his cheekbones suddenly stark and bladed.

His chocolate-brown eyes, which for the last few minutes had swirled with unreadable emotions, suddenly cleared like a whiteboard wiped clean. His face quickly returned to its set professional mask—unemotional. With his trademark abruptness, he pushed back his chair and stood.

'I have to get back to work. I'll call Monash and try and get your grandfather transported down there this afternoon for the procedure tomorrow morning. Hopefully, he'll be home by five tomorrow night.'

'Thanks, Noah.'

'Yeah.'

The terse and brooding doctor was back, front and centre, and she had the distinct feeling he'd just returned from a very dark place. 'Is everything okay?'

'Everything's just peachy,' he said sarcastically as he tossed a two-dollar coin in her direction. 'Choose a charity for the S jar.'

One side of his wide mouth pulled up wryly and she found herself wishing he'd smile again, like he had when he'd teased her about being difficult. Those rare moments of lightness were like treasured shafts of sunshine breaking through cloud on a dark and stormy day. They lit him up—a dark and damaged angel—promising the hope of redemption. His smiles made her smile. Made her feel flushed and giddy and alive. They reminded her that, despite everything, she was still a woman.

No man is who he seems. Remember Trent? He hid something so dark and dangerous from you that it exploded without warning...

And she knew that as intimately as the scars on her back and shoulder. She'd been sensible and celibate for three years without a single moment of temptation. Now wasn't the time to start craving normality—craving the touch of a man, especially not a cantankerous and melancholy guy who did little to hide his dark side.

She reminded herself very firmly that Noah would be gone in three weeks and all she had to do to stay safe and sane was to keep out of his way. He was general practice, she was midwifery. As unusual as this week had been for them to be intersecting so often at work, it was thankfully unlikely to continue.

He spun around to leave and then turned back, slapping his palm to the architrave as he often did when a thought struck him. Again, the muscles of his upper arms bulged. 'Lilia.'

A rush of tingling warmth thrummed through her. Somehow, despite his usual taciturn tone, he managed to make her full name sound soft, sweet and, oh, so feminine. 'Ye—' Her voice caught on the word, deeply husky. She cleared her throat, trying to sound in complete control instead of battling delicious but dangerous waves of arousal. 'Yes?'

'You got the agenda for the quarterly meeting at the Victoria?'

It had pinged into her inbox earlier in the day and she'd done what she always did when it arrived. Ignored it until she couldn't ignore it any longer. 'I did.'

'So you're going?'

She sighed. 'Yes. It ticks me off, though. The secretary who sets the agenda is utterly Melbourne-centric and has no clue of what's involved for people who have to travel. She always sets the meetings to start at nine in the morning, making me battle peak-hour traffic on top of a pre-dawn start.'

'So go up to Melbourne the night before,' he said reasonably.

'No.' She heard the horror in her voice and saw a flash of recognition on his face that he'd heard it too. She backpedalled fast. 'I've got a prenatal class the night before.'

'Fair enough. I'll pick you up at five, then.'

'I beg your pardon?'

He sighed. 'I can't get away early either so there's no point in both of us driving up independently. Carbon footprint, parking issues and all that.'

Panic simmered in her veins. 'I might not be able to go after all. Gramps might need me.'

He folded his arms. 'You just finished telling me there were plenty of people you can call on to keep an eye on him and this is one of those times. You know you can't miss the meeting and that it makes perfect sense for us to drive up together.'

No, no, no, no, no. She wanted to refuse his offer but she would look deranged if she insisted on driving up herself. The urge to go and rock in a corner almost overwhelmed her. She didn't know which was worse—spending two four-hour stretches in Noah's luxury but small European sports car—where there'd be no escape from his woodsy scent, his penetrating gaze and all that toned and fit masculinity—or the fact the first leg of the journey was taking her back to Melbourne, the place of her worst folly. A place full of shadows and fears where her past could appear at any moment and suck her back down into the black morass she'd fought so hard to leave.

Either way, no matter how she came at it, all of it totally sucked.

Noah opened the car door and slid back inside the warmth, surprised to find Lilia still asleep. They'd left Turraburra two hours ago in the dark, the cold and the spring fog, when the only other people likely to be awake had been insomniacs and dairy farmers.

She'd greeted him with a tight and tired smile and had immediately closed her eyes and slept. At first he'd spent far too much time glancing at her in the predawn light. Asleep, she'd lost the wary look she often wore and instead she'd looked soft and serene. And kissable. Far too kissable.

To distract himself, he'd connected his MP3 player and listened to a surgical podcast. The pressure of the looming exams was a permanent part of him and the time in the car was welcome revision time. Turraburra had kept him so busy that he hadn't found much time for study since he'd arrived, adding to his dislike of the place.

Lilia stirred, her eyes fluttering open and a sleep crease from the seat belt marking her cheek. 'What time is it?'

'Seven. I've got coffee, fruit and something the bakery calls a bear claw.'

'Yum. Thanks, that was thoughtful.'

'It's who I am,' he said, teasing her and wanting to see her smile.

'And there's another two dollars for the children's leukaemia fund,' she said with a laugh. Her usually neat braided hair was out today, flowing wildly over her shoulders. She tucked it behind her ears before accepting the coffee. 'Where are we?'

'Cranbourne.' He clicked his seat belt into place, feeling the buzz of excitement flicker into life as he pulled onto the highway and saw the sign that read 'Melbourne 60km'.

'We'll be in East Melbourne by eight-thirty with time to park and make it to the meeting by nine.'

'Great.'

The tone of her voice made him look at her. 'You just matched my donation to the sarcasm jar.'

'Who knew we were both so philanthropic,' she said caustically, before biting into her bear claw.

'Do you always wake up grumpy?'

She wiped icing sugar from her lips. 'Only when the smell of Melbourne's smog hits my nostrils.'

'Well, your bad mood isn't going to dent my enthusiasm,' he said as he changed lanes. 'I can't wait to step inside the Victoria.'

'What about sitting in snarled traffic just to get there?'

'You really are Ms Snark, aren't you?' He grinned at her, perversely enjoying the fact that their individual happiness was proportional to the proximity of their respective homes. Using it as much-needed protection and reminding himself that no matter how much his body craved her, they were a total mismatch.

'We won't be sitting in a traffic jam. I know every side street within a five-kilometre radius of the hospital. My favourite way is through Richmond.'

'That's ridiculous,' she said, her fingers suddenly shredding the white paper bag that had contained the pastry. 'That way you've got traffic lights and trams.'

He rolled his eyes. 'You've just described most of the inner city.'

'Exactly. Just *stay* on the toll road and use the tunnel,' she said tightly, her words lashing him. 'It will get us there just as fast.'

A bristle of indignation ran up his spine. 'And

suddenly the country girl's an expert on Melbourne?'

Her eyes flashed silver blue. 'On your first day I told you I did my Master's in midwifery here but you were too busy being cross to listen.'

He ignored her jibe. 'So how long did you live here?'

'Two years.' Her bitter tone clashed with the love he knew she had for midwifery and this time he did more than just glance at her. Her face had paled to the colour of the alabaster statue of mother and child that graced the foyer of MMU and her usually lush mouth had thinned to a rigid and critical line. The paper bag in her lap was now a series of narrow strips. What the hell was going on?

Don't ask. Don't get involved, remember? No emotions means no pain. Whatever's upsetting her is her thing. Let it be. It's nothing to do with you.

Her hand shot from her lap and she turned on the radio as if she too wanted to change the subject. The raucous laughter of the breakfast show announcers filled the silence between them and both of them allowed it.

Noah couldn't stop smiling as the reassuring familiarity of the Melbourne Victoria hospital wrapped around him like a child's blankie. He loved it all, from the mediocre coffee in the staff lounge to the buzz of the floor polisher being wielded by a cleaner.

The moment he'd pulled into his car space he'd been suffused with such a feeling of freedom he'd wanted to sing. Lilia, on the other hand, had looked as if she'd seen a ghost but once inside the hospital she'd perked up. They had different schedules across the day and had agreed to meet at six o'clock in the foyer. He'd gone direct to the doctors' lounge in the theatre suite like a puppy panting for a treat.

Unluckily for him, the first person he saw was Oliver Evans.

'Noah.' The surgeon greeted him coolly. 'How's Turraburra?'

It's purgatory. Certain that Oliver had been

a big part of the reason he'd been sent to the small country town, he kept his temper leashed, drawing on willpower born from his sheer determination to succeed. He was half ticked off and half grateful to the guy but, even so, he still thought that with his exams so close he could have worked on his communication skills here at the Victoria, instead of being shunted so far south.

'It's coastal. The beach is okay.'

'And the people? Emily introduced me to the midwife down there once. She seemed great.'

'She's certainly good at her job but she's seriously opinionated.'

'Not something you're known for,' Oliver said, with an accompanying eye-roll. 'She sounds like the perfect match for you.'

It was a typical comment from a happily married family man and it irked him. 'I've got exams looming, a private surgical practice to start and no interest in being matched up with anyone.'

'Shame. I remember her as intelligent, entertaining and with a good sense of humour, but then again I don't have to work with her.' He picked up a file. 'Talking about work, I imagine you're missing operating. I've got a fascinating case today if you want to scrub in and observe.'

Interest sparked. 'What is it?'

'Jeremy Watson, the paediatric cardiologist from The Deakin is inserting a stent into the heart of Flick Lawrence and Tristan Hamilton's baby. Are you in?'

Eagerness and exhilaration tumbled through him at the chance to be part of such intricate and delicate in utero surgery. He almost said, 'Hell, yeah,' but memories stopped him. Oliver standing in front of an open lift. Oliver yelling at him about a little girl with Down's syndrome. Oliver telling him to get some people skills.

This surgery wasn't taking place on just any baby—it was the unborn child of Melbourne Victoria's paediatric cardiologist. If Noah failed to acknowledge that, he knew he'd be kicked to the kerb, and fast. 'This is a pretty personal case, Oliver. Tristan and Flick are staff. How will they feel about me scrubbing in?'

Oliver gave him a long, assessing look before his stern mouth softened. 'They'll be happy to know they're in the hands of talented doctors.' He shoved papers at Noah's chest. 'Read up on the procedure so you know exactly what's required of you. We don't want Jeremy taking any stories back to The Deakin about our team not being up to scratch. I'll see you in Theatre Five at one.'

Lily's head spun after a morning of meetings. She craved to feel fresh air and sunshine on her skin instead of artificial lighting and to feel earth underneath her feet instead of being six floors up in the air. A sandwich in the park across the road from the hospital was the perfect solution.

Are you sure? What if Trent walks past?

Stop it! You're being irrational. A. Melbourne is a city of four million people. B. Trent doesn't work at the Melbourne Victoria. C. Richmond is far enough away for this not to be his local park. D. He doesn't even know you're in Melbourne and, for all you know, he might have left for Queensland, like he always said he would.

She hauled in deep breaths, trying desperately to hold onto all the logic and reason that half her brain quietly told her, while ignoring the crazy la-la her paranoia had going on. She hated that she had the same conversation with herself every time she came to Melbourne. It was one of the reasons why she limited her visits to the city to the bare minimum.

It's been three years and this has to stop. Lunch in the park will be good for you. It's the same as when you have lunch at the beach in Turraburra. You need the natural light—it will boost your serotonin and it's good for your mental health.

Still feeling jittery, she decided to take the service elevator. It gave her the best chance of making it down to the ground floor without running into anyone she knew. People who would implore her to join them for lunch in the cafeteria. She pressed the 'down' button and waited, watching the light linger on level one, the operating theatre suite.

'Lily?' Isla Delamere, looking about seven months pregnant, walked easily towards her *sans* waddle and leaned in to kiss her on the cheek. 'I thought it was you.'

Lily hugged her friend. 'Look at you. You look fantastic.'

'Thanks.' Isla rubbed her belly with a slightly distracted air. 'I'm just starting to feel a bit tired by the end of the day and Alessi has gone from dropping occasional hints that I should be giving up work to getting all macho and protective.' She laughed. 'But in a good way, you know, not a creepy way.'

Sadly, Lily understood the difference only too well. 'When do you start mat leave?'

'Next month.' A smile wreathed her face. 'I can't wait to set up the nursery and get organised.'

'That sounds like fun,' Lily said sincerely. She was shocked then to feel a flutter of something she didn't want to acknowledge as a tinge of jealousy.

The sound of voices floated out from the office—the crisp and precise tones of a female British accent contrasting sharply with a deeply male and laconic Aussie drawl. Neither voice sounded happy.

Emergencies excepted, Lily was used to the MMU being a relatively tranquil place. 'What's going on?'

'Darcie and Lucas. Again.' Isla's brows shot skyward. 'They spit and hiss like territorial cats when they get within five metres of each other. All of us are over it.' She laughed. 'We think they should just get on with it and have sex. You know, combust some of that tension so the MMU can go back to the calm place it's known for.'

Lily thought about the tension that shimmered between her and Noah and immediately felt the hot, addictive heaviness between her legs. 'You really think having sex would work?'

'I have no clue but if it means Darcie and Lucas could work together in harmony, I'd say do it. They'd make an amazing obstetric team.'

Working in harmony...

Stop it! Now you're totally losing your mind. Don't even go there.

'You okay, Lily?' Isla asked, clicking her fingers. 'You've vagued out on me.'

She forced a laugh. 'Sorry, I was thinking about sex and the occupational health and safety implications.'

'As long as no ladders are involved, it's probably fine,' Isla quipped, then her face sobered. 'Lily, if you're not busy, can you do me a favour?'

You really need ten minutes in the park out of this artificial light so you can get through the rest of the day. The thought of being in the park and Trent finding her there sent her heart into panicky overdrive. 'I'm not busy, Isla. How can I help?'

'I hate this so much, Lily.' Tristan Hamilton leaned his head against the glass that separated them from Theatre Five, gazing down at his wife's draped and prostrate form on the operating table. The only thing not covered in green was Flick's pregnant belly.

'It must be so hard.' Lily put her hand on the

Melbourne Victoria's neonatal cardiothoracic surgeon's shoulder, struck by the sobering thought that today he wasn't a doctor, just a scared and anxious father-to-be. 'It's especially difficult when you're the one used to being in charge and in control so let's look at the positives. Oliver's an expert in utero surgeon and you and Jeremy Watson share that award for the ground-breaking surgery the two of you did on the conjoined twins. Just like you, he's one of the best. Flick and the baby are in great hands.'

Isla had explained to Lily how she'd desperately wanted to support both Tristan and Flick by being here and how she and Alessi had discussed it. They'd both felt strongly that it would be difficult enough to cope with the fact their baby was undergoing life-threatening surgery without their support person being heavily pregnant with a healthy baby. Isla had asked Lily to stay with Tristan throughout the operation, saying, 'He says he doesn't need anyone with him but he does, and you're perfect because you're always so calm.'

Lily had immediately thought about her chaotic reactions to Noah, which were the antithesis of calm, but she hadn't voiced them because it hadn't been the time or place. People needed her. They needed her to be the person they thought she was—serene and unflappable. No one knew how hard she'd worked to cultivate that aura of tranquillity for her own protection.

Now she was doing as Isla asked, staying with Tristan during the surgery, and she was glad. The guy was understandably stressed and she was more than happy to help.

The operating theatre was full of people scrubbed and wearing green gowns, unflattering blue paper hats and pale blue-green masks. Their only visible distinguishing features were their eyes and stance. She recognised Ed Yang, the anaesthetist, by his almond-shaped eyes, Oliver Evans's by his wide-legged stance, and Jeremy Watson by his short stature and nimble movments, but she didn't recognise the back of the taller doctor standing next to him.

'Oliver is using ultrasound to guide Jeremy's large-gauge needle into Flick's abdomen. It will pierce the uterus before going directly into the baby's heart,' Tristan said, as if he was conducting a teaching session for the interns.

If talking was going to help him get through this then Lily was more than happy to listen.

'Of course the risks are,' he continued in a low voice, 'rupture of the amniotic sac, bleeding through the insertion site, the baby's heart bleeding into the pericardial sac and compressing the heart.' His voice cracked. 'And death.'

Lily slid her hand into his and squeezed it hard. 'And the best-case scenario is the successful insertion of the stent and a healthy baby born at term.'

'Who will still need more surgery.'

Lily heard the guilt and sadness in his voice. 'But the baby will be strong enough to cope with it. Most importantly, unlike you, he or she is unlikely to need a heart transplant. You know it's a different world now from when you were born and your baby is extremely fortunate to have the best doctors in the country.'

'You're right. She is.' He gave her a grateful smile. 'We're having a little girl. We found out during the tests.'

'That's so exciting.'

'It is.' A slow smile wove across his face. 'I thought I didn't need anyone here with me today but I was wrong. Thanks for being here, Lily.'

'Oh, Tris, it's an honour. All I ask is for a big cuddle when she's born.'

'It's a deal.' He suddenly muttered something that sounded like, 'Thank God.'

'Tris?'

He grinned at her. 'The stent's in. Both my girls have come through the surgery with flying colours.'

'Fantastic.' She noticed the assistant surgeon suddenly raising both of his arms away from the surgical field as if he were a victim of an armed hold-up. He stepped back from the table. 'What's happening?'

'That's the surgical registrar. The operation's almost over and he's not required any more.'

As the unknown surgeon walked around, he glanced up at the glass. A set of very familiar brown eyes locked with hers. She stifled a gasp. *Noah.*

The Swiss chocolate colour of his eyes was familiar but she didn't recognise anything else about them. Gone was the serious, slightly mocking expression that normally resided there and in its place was unadulterated joy. His eyes positively sparkled, like fireworks on New Year's Eve.

Her heart kicked up, her knees sagged and lust wound down into every part of her, urging her dormant body to wake up. Wake up and dare to take a risk—live on the wild side and embrace it—like she'd often done before life with Trent had extinguished that part of her.

No. Not safe. You must stay safe.

Panic closed her eyes but the vision of his elation stayed with her—vibrant and full of life—permanently fused to her mind like a brand.

It scared the hell out of her.

CHAPTER FIVE

'MAN, THAT WAS a great day,' Noah said, smoothly changing through the gears as he took yet another bend on the narrow, winding and wet road back to Turraburra.

'I'm glad,' Lilia said with a quiet smile in her voice.

'Why?'

She sighed. 'Are you always so suspicious of someone being happy for you?'

He glanced at her quickly before returning his gaze to the rainy night, the windscreen wipers working overtime to keep the windshield clear. 'Sorry, but you have to admit we don't exactly get along.'

'That's true, I guess, but today I saw you in a new light.'

‘Should I be worried?’ he said, half teasing, half concerned.

‘I guess I saw you on your home turf and I’ve never seen you look like that before. You looked happy.’ Her fingers tangled with each other on her lap. ‘You’ve really missed the Victoria and surgery, haven’t you?

‘Like an amputee misses his leg.’ He shot her an appreciative glance, one part of him both happy and surprised that she’d drawn the connections. ‘Couldn’t you feel the vibe of the place? Being part of world-class surgery is my adrenalin rush.

‘It bubbles in my veins and I love it. What you saw today, when Jeremy inserted that stent into the Hamilton-Lawrence baby’s heart, is cutting-edge stuff. It’s an honour and a privilege to be part of it and I want to be part of it. I didn’t work this hard for this long to spend my life stuck in a backwater.’

‘Let me take a wild stab in the dark that you’re talking about a place like Turraburra.’

‘Exactly. By the way, you owe another two dollars to the S jar,’ he said lightly, then he sobered.

'But, seriously, doesn't it frustrate you on some level that you're so far away from the centre of things?'

'Not at all,' she said emphatically, the truth in her voice ringing out loud and clear in the darkness of the car.

'I can't believe you didn't even have to think about that for a second.'

'How is it any different from me asking you if being in Melbourne frustrates you on any level?'

He nodded thoughtfully. 'Fair point.'

'Noah, babies have been coming into the world in pretty much the same way for thousands of years so, for me, the joy comes from helping women, not from feeling the need to be constantly chasing new and exciting ways of doing things.'

He thought of his mother. 'There's nothing wrong with wanting to discover new techniques and new ways of doing things. It's how we progress, find cures for diseases, better ways of treating people.'

'I never said there was anything wrong with it.'

She suddenly pointed out the window and yelled, 'Wombat! Look out.'

His headlights picked up the solid black shape in the rain, standing stock-still on the road, right in the path of the car. He pulled the steering-wheel hard, swerving to avoid hitting and instantly killing the marsupial. Lilia's hands gripped the dash, stark white in the dark as the car heaved left. The tyres hit the gravel edge of the road and the car fishtailed wildly.

Don't do this. He braked, trying to pull the car back under control, but in the wet it had taken on its own unstoppable trajectory. The back wheels, unable to grip the gravel, skidded and the next moment the car pulled right, sliding across the white lines to the wrong side of the road. White posts and trees came at them fast and he hauled the wheel the other way, driving on instinct, adrenalin and fear.

The car suddenly spun one hundred and eighty degrees and stopped, coming to an abrupt halt and facing in the opposite direction from where they were headed. The headlights picked up shadows, the trees and the incessant rain, tumbling down from the sky like a wall of water. The wombat ambled in front of the car and disappeared into the bushes.

Noah barely dared to breathe while he did a mental checklist that all his body parts still moved and that he was indeed, alive. When reality pierced his terror, his half-numb fingers clumsily released his seat belt and he leaned towards Lilia, grabbing her shoulder. 'Are you okay?'

'I…I…' Her voice wobbled in the darkness. 'I thought for sure we'd slam into the trees. I thought we were dead.'

'So did I.' He flicked on the map reading light, needing to see her.

Her eyes stared back at him, wide and enormous, their blue depths obliterated by huge black discs. 'But we're not.'

'No.' He raised his right hand to her cheek, needing to touch her, needing to feel that she was in one piece. 'We're safe.'

'Safe.' She breathed out the word before wrapping her left hand tightly around his forearm as if she needed to hold onto something.

Her heat and sheer relief collided with his, calling to him, and he dropped his head close in to hers, capturing her lips in a kiss of reassurance. A kiss of mutual comfort that they'd survived unscathed. That they were fine and here to live another day.

Her lips were warm, pliant and, oh, so gloriously soft. As he brushed his lips gently against them, he tasted salt and sugar. God, he wanted to delve deep and taste more. Feel more.

He suddenly became aware she'd stilled. She was neither leaning into the kiss nor leaning back. She was perfectly motionless and for a brief moment he thought he should pull away—that his kiss was unwelcome—but then she made a raw sound in the back of her throat. Half moan, half groan, it tore through him like a primal force, igniting ten long days of suppressed desire.

He slid one hand gently around her neck, cupping the back of it and tilting her head. He deepened the kiss while he used his other hand to release her seat belt. Her arms immediately slid up around his neck and she met his kiss with one of her own.

If he'd expected hesitation and uncertainty, he'd been wrong. Her tongue frantically explored his mouth as if she had only one chance to do so, branding him with her heat and her taste, and setting him alight in a way he'd never known. His blood pounded need and desire through him hot and fast, and his breathing came short and ragged. He wanted to touch her and feel her, wanted her to touch and feel him. Hell, he just wanted her.

His talented surgical fingers, usually so nimble and controlled, fumbled with the buttons on her blouse. Lilia didn't even try to undo his buttons—she just ripped. Designer buttons flew everywhere and then her palms pressed against his skin, searing him. Her lips followed, tracing a direct line along his chest to his nipples. Her tongue flicked. Silver spots danced before his eyes.

Somehow he managed to rasp out, 'Need more

room.' Shooting his seat back, he hauled her over him. As she straddled him, her thighs pressed against his legs and she leaned forward, lowering her mouth to his again. Her hair swung, forming a curtain around their heads, encasing them in a blonde cocoon and isolating them from the real world. It was wild and crazy as elbows and knees collided with windows, the steering-wheel and the handbrake. A small part of him expected her to jolt back to sanity, pull back and scramble off him.

Thank God, it didn't happen.

He'd never been kissed like it. She lurched from ingénue to moments of total control. Her mouth burned hot on his and her body quivered against him, driving him upward to breaking point. She matched his every move with one of her own, and when he finally managed to unhook her bra she whipped off his belt. When he slid his hand under her skirt, caressing the skin of her inner thighs, she undid his fly. When he cupped her, she gripped him.

She rose above him a glorious Amazon—face

flushed, eyes huge, full breasts heaving—and he wanted nothing more than to watch her fly. 'God, you're amazing.'

'Shush.' Lilia managed to sound the warning. She didn't want compliments, she didn't want conversation—she didn't want to risk anything being said that might make her think beyond this moment. She'd spent years living a safe and bland life and tonight she could have died. In this moment she needed to feel alive in a way she hadn't felt in years. The woman she'd once been—the one life had subjugated—broke through, demanding to be heard. She had Noah under her, his hands on her, and she was taking everything he offered.

'No condoms,' he said huskily. 'Sorry. Hope this will do.' His thumb rotated gently on her clitoris as his fingers slid inside her, moving back and forth with delicious and mind-blowing pressure.

She swayed against him, her hands moving on him trying to return the favour, but under his deft and targeted ministrations they fell away. Sensations built inside her, drowning out everything until nothing existed at all except pleasure. Sheer, glorious, pleasure. It caught her, pushing her upwards, pulling her forward, and spinning her out on an axis of wonder until she exploded in a shower of light far, far away from everything that tied her to her life.

As she drifted back to earth, muscles twitching, chest panting, she caught his sparkling eyes and deliciously self-satisfied grin.

What have you done?

The enormity of what had just happened hit her like a truck, sucking the breath from her lungs and scaring her rigid.

If Lily hadn't known better she would have said she'd drunk a lot of tequila and today's headache was the result of a hangover. Only she knew she hadn't touched a drop of alcohol yesterday or today. All she wanted was to desperately forget everything about last night's drive home from Melbourne, but sadly it was all vividly crystal clear, including her screaming Noah's name when she'd come.

She ruffled her dog's ears. 'Oh, Chippy, I've been so sensible and restrained for so long, why did I have to break last night? Break with Noah?'

But break she had—spectacularly. How could she have put herself at risk like that? Left herself open to so many awful possibilities?

It was Noah, not a mass murderer.

We don't know that.

Oh, come on!

She blamed Isla's suggestion that people should have sex to defuse tension, Noah's look of utter joy in the operating theatre, which had reached out and deliciously wrapped around her, and finally, to cap it all off, their near-death experience. All of it had combined, making her throw caution to the wind. But despite how she was trying to justify her actions, the only person she could blame was herself. She'd spent all night wide awake, doing exactly that.

Gramps had even commented at breakfast that she looked in worse shape than he did. Since the insertion of his pacemaker he was doing really well and had a lot more energy than he'd had in a long time. For that she was grateful. She was also grateful that she hadn't seen Noah all morning.

Last night, after she'd scrambled off his lap in a blind panic and had said, 'Don't say a word, just drive,' he'd done exactly that. When he'd pulled up at the house just before eleven, he'd leaned in to kiss her on the cheek. She'd managed to duck him and had hopped out of the car fast. Using the door as a barrier between them, she'd thanked him for the ride and had tried to walk normally to the front door when every part of her had wanted to run. Run from the fact she'd just had sex in a car.

Dear God, she was twenty-nine years old and old enough to know better. She'd kept the wild side of herself boxed up for years and she still couldn't believe she'd allowed it to surface. Not when she had the physical evidence on her body constantly reminding her of the danger it put her in.

She lined her pens up in a row on her desk

and straightened the files in her in-box. Yesterday was just a bump in the road of her life and today everything went back to normal. Normal, just like it had been for the last three years. Like she needed it to be. Safe. Controlled. Restrained. Absolutely drama-free.

A hysterical laugh rose in her throat. She should probably text Isla, telling her that sex didn't reduce tension at all. If anything, it made things ten times worse.

She dropped her head in her hands. She had to work with Noah for the next two and a half weeks and all the time he would know that if he tried, it barely took any time at all for him to strip away her reserve and reduce her to a primal mess of quivering and whimpering need. She'd unwittingly given him power over her—power she'd vowed no man would ever have over her again. Somehow she had to get through seventeen days before she could breathe easily again.

To keep her chaotic thoughts from ricocheting all over her brain, she decided to check her inventory for expired sterilised equipment and drugs nearing their use-by dates. There was nothing like order and routine to induce calm.

She was halfway through the job when a knock on her door made her turn.

'May I come in?'

Noah stood in the doorway in his characteristic pose of one hand pressed against the doorjamb, only this time he looked very different. Gone was the suit and tie he'd worn during his first week and a half in Turraburra. Today his long legs were clad in chinos and his chest, which she now knew was rock-hard muscle, was covered in a green, pink, blue and orange striped casual shirt. His brown curls bounced and his eyes danced. He looked…relaxed.

Her heart leaped, her blood pounded and tingles of desire slammed through her, making her shimmer from top to toe. If her body had been traitorously attracted to the strung-out Noah, it was nothing compared to its reaction to the relaxed Noah.

Distance. Keep your distance. 'I'm pretty busy, Noah. Did you need something?'

His mouth curved up in a genuine smile that raced to his eyes. 'I figured, seeing as we've done things back to front and had sex first, we should probably go out to dinner.'

'I...I don't think that's a good idea,' she said hurriedly, before her quivering body overrode her common sense and she accepted the unexpected invitation. 'And we didn't actually have sex,' she said, feeling mortified that she'd been the one to have the orgasm while he'd been left hanging.

His brows rose. 'I'm pretty certain what we did comes under the banner of sex.'

The irony of what she'd said wasn't lost on her, given she always put a lot of emphasis in sex ed classes with the local teenagers on the fact that sex wasn't just penetration. 'Either way, it was a mistake so why compound it by going on a date?'

'A mistake?' The words came out tinged with offence and a flare of hurt momentarily sparked in his eyes before fading fast. 'If it was a mistake, why did you have sex with me?'

She didn't meet his gaze. 'I panicked.'

'You panicked?'

She heard the incredulity in his voice and it added to the flash of hurt she'd seen. She felt bad and it made her tell him the truth. 'I'd just had a near-death experience and I hadn't had sex in a very long time.'

'So you used me?'

Her head jerked up at the slight edge in his voice. 'Oh, and you didn't use me?'

A look of distaste and utter indignation slid across his face and two red spots appeared on his cheeks as if she'd slapped him. 'No! I don't use women. What the hell sort of a man do you think I am?'

A kernel of guilt burrowed into her that because of Trent's role in her life she'd offended him, but she wasn't about to explain to him why. 'Look, we're adults. You don't need to appease your conscience by buying me dinner. What happened happened and now we can just forget about it and move on.'

'I don't want to forget about it,' he said softly, as he moved towards her.

Panic had her pulling a linen skip between

them but he put his hands on either side of it and leaned in close. 'Do you?'

His soft words wound down into her, taunting her resolve. *I have to forget.*

He suddenly straightened up and opened his hands out palms upward in supplication. 'Come to dinner, Lily. You never know, we might actually enjoy each other's company.'

'I really don't think—'

'I promise you it will just be dinner.' He gave a wry smile. 'Sex is an optional extra and totally your choice. I'm not here to talk you into or out of it.'

She stared at him, trying desperately hard to read him and coming up blank. Why was he was doing this? Why was he being so nice? She sought signs of calculation but all she could see was genuineness. It clashed with everything she wanted to believe about him—about all men—only she got a sense that if she said no, she'd offend him. Again. 'Okay, but I'm paying.'

His jaw stiffened. 'I'm not an escort service. We'll go Dutch.'

The memory of him stroking her until she'd come made her cheeks burn hotly. 'I guess… um…that's fair.'

Shoving his hands in his pockets, he said, 'I'd offer to pick you up but that would probably upset your independent sensibilities. Emergencies and babies excepted, how does seven at Casuarina sound?'

She was so rusty at accepting invitations that her voice came out all scratchy. 'Seven sounds good.'

He shot her a wary smile. 'Cheer up. You never know, you might just enjoy yourself.'

Before she could say another word, he'd turned and left.

Please, let a baby be born tonight. Please.

But, given her luck with men, that was probably not going to happen.

CHAPTER SIX

NOAH FULLY EXPECTED Lily to cancel. Every email and text that had hit his phone during the afternoon he'd opened with that thought first and foremost in his mind. Now, as he sat alone in the small restaurant, he fingered his phone, turning it over and over, still waiting for the call to come. He caught sight of his countdown app and opened it. Four hundred and fifty-six hours left in Turraburra. Almost halfway.

Why are you even here in this restaurant? That thought had been running concurrently with *She will cancel.* He had no clue why he'd insisted they have dinner. It wasn't like he'd never taken the gift of casual sex before and walked away without a second glance. Granted, he'd not actually hit the end zone last night, but watching Lilia shatter above him had brought him pretty damn close. And it had felt good in a way he hadn't experienced in a long time.

Something about her—the wildness in the way she'd kissed him, the desperation in the way she'd come and then her rapid retreat into herself afterwards had kick-started something in him. A desire to get to know her more. A vague caring—something he'd put on ice years ago.

It confused him and dinner had seemed a way of exorcising both the confusion and the caring. Hell, her reaction to his dinner invitation had almost nuked the caring on the spot. He'd never had a woman so reluctant to accept his invitation and it had fast become a challenge to get her to accept. He refused to be relegated to the category of *a mistake.* He checked his watch. Seven-ten p.m.

'Would you like a drink, Dr Jackson?' Georgia Brady asked, as she extended the black-bound wine list towards him.

Noah had recently prescribed the contraceptive

pill for the young woman and had conducted the examination that went along with that. He was slightly taken aback to find she was now his waitress. 'I think I'll wait, thanks.'

'Who are you waiting for?'

'Lilia Cartwright,' he answered, before he realised the inappropriateness of the question. Small towns with their intense curiosity were so not his thing. 'Aren't there other customers needing your attention?'

Georgia laughed as she indicated the virtually empty restaurant. 'Thursday nights in Turraburra are pretty quiet. Are you sure Lily's coming? It's just she never dates.'

'It's a work dinner,' he said quickly, as a crazy need to protect Lilia from small-town gossip slugged him.

Georgia nodded. 'That makes more sense. Oh, here she is. Hi, Lily.'

Lily stood in the entrance of the restaurant and slipped off her coat, wondering for the thousandth time why she was there. Why she hadn't created an excuse to cancel. That was the one drawback of a small town. Without a cast-iron reason it was, oh, so easy to be caught out in a lie because everybody knew what everyone was doing and when they were doing it. So, here she was. She'd eat and leave. An hour, max.

Plastering on a smile, she walked forward and said, 'Hi, Georgia,' as she took her seat opposite Noah, who'd jumped to his feet on her arrival. 'Noah.'

He gave her a nod and she thought he looked as nervous as she felt.

'If this is a work dinner, will you want wine?' Georgia asked.

'Yes.'

Noah spoke at exactly the same moment as she did, his deep 'Yes' rolling over hers.

They both laughed tightly and Georgia gave them an odd look before going to fetch the bottle of Pinot Gris Noah ordered.

Lily fiddled with her napkin. 'This is a work dinner?'

Noah grimaced. 'Georgia was giving me the

third degree about my date and as the town believes you're married to your job, I thought it best not to disabuse them.'

She stared at him, stunned. 'How do you know the town thinks I'm married to my job?'

'Linda Sampson told me on my first day,' he said matter-of-factly, before sipping some water. 'So are you?'

She didn't reply until Georgia had finished pouring the wine, placed the bottle in an ice bucket by the side of the table and left. 'I love my job but I also love Gramps, Chippy and bush-walking. Plus, I'm involved as a volunteer with Coastcare so I live a very balanced life,' she said, almost too emphatically. 'It's just that Linda wants to marry off every single woman in town.'

'And man,' Noah said, with a shake of his head. 'The first day I was here she ran through a list of possible candidates for me, despite the fact I'd told her I wasn't looking.'

'Why aren't you looking?' The question came out before she'd censored it.

His perceptive gaze hooked hers. 'Why aren't you?'

So not going there. She dropped her gaze and sipped the wine, savouring the flavours of pear and apple as they zipped along her tongue. 'This is lovely.'

'I like it. The Bellarine Peninsula has some great wineries.'

'You mean there are times you actually leave Melbourne voluntarily?' she teased.

He grinned. 'I've been known to when wine's involved.'

'There's a winery an hour away from here.'

'This far south?'

She smiled at his scepticism. 'They only make reds but the flavours are really intense. You should visit. You get great wine, amazing views across Wilson's Prom and wedge-tailed eagles.'

His eyes, always so serious, lightened in self-deprecation. 'I guess I should have read the tourist information they sent me after all.'

She raised her glass. 'To the hidden gems of Turraburra.'

'And to finding them.' He clinked her glass with his, his gaze skimming her from the top of her forehead, across her face and down to her breasts and back again.

A shiver of need thundered through her and she hastily crossed her legs against the intense throb, trying to quash it. She gulped her wine, quickly draining the glass and then regretting it as the alcohol hit her veins.

Stick to pleasantries. 'The eye fillet here is locally grown and so tender it melts in your mouth.'

'Sounds good to me,' he said, as he instructed Georgia that he wanted his with the blood stopped. When the waitress had refilled their glasses, removed the menus and departed for the kitchen, he said, 'I saw your grandfather this morning for his check-up. He's a new man.'

'He is. Thanks.'

He gave a wry smile. 'Don't thank me. Thank the surgeon who inserted the pacemaker and fixed the problem.'

'A typical surgeon's response. Noah, you made the diagnosis so please accept the thanks.' She fiddled with the base of her glass and sought desperately for something to say that was neutral. 'So you know I grew up in Turraburra, what about you?'

He took a long drink of his wine.

Her curiosity ramped up three notches. 'Is it a secret?'

'No. It's just not very interesting.'

'Try me.'

'West of Sydney.'

She thought about his reaction to Turraburra and wondered if he'd grown up in a small town. 'How west? Orange? Cowra?'

'Thankfully, not that far west.' He ran his hand through his curls as if her questions hurt. 'I grew up in a poverty-stricken, gossip-ridden town on the edge of Sydney. Not really country but too far away to be city. I hated it and I spent most of my teenage years plotting to get out and stay out.'

She thought about her own childhood—of the freedom of the beach, of the love of her grandfather and the circle of care from the town—and she felt sad for him. 'Do your parents still live there?'

He shook his head. 'I was a change-of-life baby. Totally unexpected and my mother was forty-four when she had me. They're both dead now.'

She knew all about that. 'I'm sorry.'

'Don't be.'

The harshness of his reply shocked her. 'You're glad your parents are dead?'

A long sigh shuddered out of him and he suddenly looked haggard and tired. 'Of course not, but I'm glad they're no longer suffering.'

'So they didn't die from old age?'

'Not exactly.' He cut through the steak Georgia had quietly placed in front of him. 'My father died breathless and drowning in heart failure and my mother…' He bit harshly into the meat.

His pain washed over Lily and she silently reached out her hand, resting it on top of his. He stared at it for a moment before swallowing. 'She died a long and protracted death from amyotrophic lateral sclerosis.'

Motor neurone disease. 'Oh, God, that must

have been awful.' She caught a flash of gratitude in his eyes that she understood. 'Did you have a good nursing home?'

'At the very end we did but for the bulk of two years I cared for her at home.' His thumb moved slowly against her hand, almost unconsciously, caressing her skin in small circular motions.

Delicious sensations wove through her, making her mind cloud at the edges. She forced herself to concentrate, working hard to hear him rather than allowing herself to follow the bliss. 'That's…that's a long time to care for someone.'

His mouth flattened into a grim line as he nodded his agreement. 'It is and, to be honest, when I took the job on we didn't have a diagnosis. I just assumed she'd need a bit of help for a while until she got stronger. I had no clue it would play out like it did, and had I known I might have…'

She waited a beat but he didn't say anything so she waded right on in. 'When did she get sick?'

'When I was nineteen. With illness, no timing is ever good but this totally sucked. I was living in Coogee by the beach, doing first-year medicine at UNSW and loving my life. It was step one of my plan to get out and stay out of Penrington.'

She thought of what he'd said about growing up in a poverty-stricken town. 'Because doctors are rarely unemployed?'

'That and the fact I was sixteen when my father died. I guess it's an impressionable age and I used to daydream that if I'd been a doctor I could have saved him.' He gave a snort of harsh laughter. 'Of course, I now know that no doctor could have changed the outcome, but at the time it was a driving force for me to choose medicine as a career.'

A stab of guilt pierced her under the ribs. She'd so easily assigned him the role of arrogant surgeon—a guy who'd chosen the prestigious speciality for the money—that she'd missed his altruism. 'You must have needed a lot of help to balance the demands of your study with helping your mum.'

He shook his head. 'My parents never had a lot of money and Mum gave up work to care for Dad in his last weeks of life. By the time she got sick, there wasn't any spare cash for a paid carer and there wasn't a lot of choice.'

'What did you do?'

He pulled his hand away from hers and ripped open the bread roll, jerkily applying butter. 'I deferred uni at the end of first year and took care of her.'

She thought about her own egocentric student days. 'That would have been a huge life change.'

His breath came out in a hiss. 'Tell me about it. I went from the freedom of uni where life consisted of lectures and parties to being stuck back in Penrington, which I'd thought I'd escaped. Only this time I was basically confined to the house. I spent a lot of time being angry and the rest of it feeling hellishly guilty as I watched my strong and capable mother fade in front of me.'

There weren't many nineteen-year-olds who'd take on full-time care like that and this was Noah. Noah, who seemed so detached and closed off from people. She struggled to wrap her head around it. 'But surely you had some help?'

He shrugged. 'The council sent a cleaner every

couple of weeks and a nurse would visit three times a week, you know the drill, but the bulk of her care fell to me.' He took a gulp of the wine before looking at her, his eyes filled with anguish. 'Every day I was haunted by a thousand thoughts. Would she choke on dinner? Would she aspirate food into her lungs? Would she fall? Would she wake up in the morning?'

Lily heard the misery and grief in his voice and her heart wept. This brisk, no-nonsense, shoot-from-the-hip doctor—the man who seemed to have great difficulty empathising with patients—had nursed his mother. 'I… That's… It…'

'Shocks you, doesn't it?' he said drily, accurately gauging her reaction. 'Part of it shocks me too but life has a way of taking you to places you never expected to go.'

He returned to eating his meal and she ate some of hers, giving him a chance to take a break from his harrowing story. She was certain he'd use the opportunity to change the subject and she knew she'd let him. She was familiar with how hard it was to revisit traumatic memories, so it came as a surprise when he continued.

'You really don't learn a lot more than anatomy and some physiology in first-year medicine and I truly believed we'd find a doctor who could help Mum.' His hand sneaked back to hers, covering it with his warmth. 'We went from clinic to clinic, saw specialist after specialist, tried three different drug trials and nothing changed except that Mum continued to deteriorate. In all those months, not one person ever said it was hopeless and that there was no cure.' His mouth curled. 'I've never forgiven them for that.'

'And yet you still had enough faith to return to your studies and qualify as a doctor?'

'I became a surgeon,' he said quietly but vehemently. 'Surgery's black and white. I see a problem and I can either fix it or I can't. And that's what I tell my patients. I give it to them straight and I *never* give them false hope.'

And there it was—the reason he was so direct. She'd been totally wrong about him. It wasn't deliberate rudeness—it came from a heartfelt place, only the message got lost in translation and came out harsh and uncaring. 'There's a middle line between false hope and stark truth, Noah,' she said quietly, hoping he'd actually hear her message.

He pulled his hand away. 'Apparently so.'

Her hand felt sadly cool and she struggled not to acknowledge how much she missed his touch.

Noah helped Lily into her coat, taking advantage of the moment to breathe in deeply and inhale her perfume. All too soon, her coat was on and it was time for him to open the front door of Casuarina and follow her outside onto the esplanade. The rhythmic boom of the waves against the sand enveloped them and he had to admit it had a soothing quality. He glanced along the street. 'Where's your car?'

She thrust her hands into her coat pockets, protecting them against the spring chill. 'I walked.'

'I've got mine. I can drive you home.'

Her eyes widened for a second and he caught the moment she recalled exactly what had happened the last time they had been in his car. Sex.

The topic they'd both gone to great lengths to avoid talking about tonight. The one thing he'd told her was her choice.

He didn't want her to bolt home alone so he hastily amended his offer. 'Or I can walk you home, if you prefer.'

She tilted her head and studied him as if she couldn't quite work him out and then she gave him a smile full of gratitude. 'Thanks. A walk would be great.'

'A walk it is, then.' She could go from guardedly cautious to sexy in a heartbeat and it disarmed him, leaving him wondering and confused. With one of her hands on her hip, he took advantage of an opportunity to touch her and slid his arm through hers. 'Which way?'

She glanced at his arm as if she was considering if she should allow it to remain there but she didn't pull away. 'Straight ahead.'

The darkness enveloped them as they strolled out of the pool of light cast by the streetlamp. Unlike Melbourne, there weren't streetlights every few houses—in fact, once you left the main street and the cluster of shops on the esplanade there were very few lights. He glanced up into the bright and cluttered Milky Way. 'The stars are amazing here.'

'The benefits of barely any light pollution. Are you interested in astronomy?'

He mused over the question. 'I'm not saying I'm not interested, it's just I've never really given it much thought.'

'Too busy working and studying?'

'You got it.'

She directed them across the street and produced a torch from her pocket as they turned into an unpaved road. 'How far away are you from taking your final exams?'

'Six months,' he said, trying really hard to sound neutral instead of bitter and avoid yet another city-versus-country argument.

She stopped walking so suddenly that his continued motion pulled her into his chest and her torch blinded him. 'What's wrong? Did you leave something at the restaurant?' he asked, seeing floaters as he turned off the torch.

'Six months?' Her voice rose incredulously. 'That close?' Her hands gripped his forearms. 'Noah, you should be in Melbourne.'

Her unexpected support flowed into him. 'You won't get an argument from me.'

'So why are you here?'

Her voice came out of the dark, asking the same question she'd posed almost two weeks ago. Back then he'd dodged it, not wanting to tell her the truth. Admitting to frailties wasn't something he enjoyed doing. Then again, he hadn't told anyone in a very long time about the dark days of caring for his mother and although he'd initially been reluctant, telling Lily the story at dinner hadn't been the nightmare he'd thought it would be.

Don't expose weakness.

She'll understand.

Hell, she'd hinted at dinner that she suspected so what was the point in avoiding the question? He sucked in a deep breath of sea air and found his fingers playing with strands of her hair. 'The chief of surgery believes if I sat the communication component of my exams now, I'd fail. He sent me down here for a massive increase in patient contact when they're awake.'

Her fingers ran along the lapel of his jacket and then she took the torch back from him, turning it on. Light spilled around them. 'Do you think you're improving?'

God, he hoped so. He'd been trying harder than he ever had before but it didn't come easily. 'What do you think?'

She worried her bottom lip.

He groaned as his blood pounded south. 'Lily, please don't do that unless you want me to kiss you.'

'Sorry.'

Her voice held an unusual trace of anxious apology, which immediately snagged him. 'Don't be sorry. But, seriously, do you think I'd pass now?'

She sighed. 'Do you promise not to yell?'

'Come on, Lily,' he said bewildered, 'I'm asking for your opinion. Why would I yell?'

She gave a strangled laugh. 'Because what I'm about to say may not be what you want to hear.'

He gently tucked her hair behind her ears, wanting to reassure her. 'I've been watching you for a week and a half and you have a natural gift with people. I want and need your opinion.'

She was quiet for a moment and when she spoke her voice was soft and low. 'I think you're doing better than when you arrived.'

Her tone did little to reassure him. 'But?'

'But you're not quite there yet.'

Damn it. Every part of him tightened in despair and he ploughed his hands through his hair. He'd thought what he was doing was enough and now that he knew it wasn't, he had no clue what else he could try.

She reached up, her hand touching his cheek. 'I can help, Noah.'

The warmth of her hand dived into him, only this time, along with arousal, came something else entirely. He didn't know how to describe it but hope was tangled up in it. 'How?'

Her hand dropped away and she recommenced walking as if she'd regretted the intimate touch. 'It's no different from surgery.'

'It's hugely different from surgery,' he said, nonplussed.

'I meant,' she said kindly, 'it's a skill you can learn.'

'And you're willing to teach me? Why?'

She paused outside a house whose veranda lamp threw out a warm, golden glow. When she looked up at him he caught a war of emotions in her eyes and on her pursed lips. 'Because, Noah, despite not wanting to and despite all logic, I like you.'

He should be affronted but the words made him smile. 'Aw, you're such a sweet talker,' he teased. 'Does this mean I'm no longer a mistake?'

She tensed. 'Goodnight, Noah.'

Crazy disappointment filled him that she was going to turn and disappear inside. He wasn't ready to let her go just yet. 'Lily, wait. I'm sorry.' He wanted her back in his arms and to kiss her goodnight but he had the distinct impression that if he pulled her towards him she'd pull right back. The woman who'd thrown caution to the wind last night had vanished like a desert mirage.

He shot for honesty. 'I had a good time tonight.'

She fiddled with her house key. 'So did I. Thanks.'

'You're welcome.' He suddenly gave in to an overwhelming urge to laugh.

Her chin instantly jutted. 'What's so funny?'

'This.' He threw out his arms, indicating the space between them. 'A first date after we've touched each other in amazing places and I've almost come just watching you fall apart over me. Yet I'm standing here on your grandfather's veranda like an inexperienced teenager, wondering if I'm allowed to kiss you goodnight.'

Her feet shuffled, her heels tapping on the wooden boards. 'You still want to kiss me, even though you know nothing else is going to happen?'

Something in her quiet voice made goosebumps rise on his arms. 'Lily, what's going on?'

'Nothing. Just checking.'

The words came out so sharply they whipped him. The last thing he expected was for her to step in close, wrap her arms around him, rise up on her toes and press her lips to his.

But he wasn't complaining. His arms tightened around her as he opened his mouth under hers. Orange and dark chocolate rushed him, tempting him, addicting him, and he moaned softly as his blood thundered pure pleasure through his veins. It hit his legs and he sat heavily on the veranda ledge of the old Californian bungalow, pulling her in close, loving the feel of her breasts and belly pressing against him.

She explored his mouth like a sailor in uncharted waters—flicking and probing, marking territory—each touch setting fire to a new part of him until he was one united blaze, existing only for her. The frenzied exploration slowly faded and with one deep kiss she stole the breath from his lungs.

A moment later, wild-eyed and panting, she swung out of his arms and opened the front door.

'Lily,' he croaked, barely able to see straight and struggling to construct a coherent sentence, 'not that I'm complaining, but somehow I think I still owe you a kiss.'

A wan smile lifted the edge of her mouth. 'Not at all. Goodnight, Noah.'

As the door clicked shut softly, he had the craziest impression that he'd just passed some sort of a test.

CHAPTER SEVEN

LILY CLOSED THE DOOR behind her and sagged back against it.

What on earth were you thinking?

I wasn't thinking at all.

And that was the problem. What had started out as a kiss to test if what Noah had said about sex being her choice was really true had almost culminated in something else entirely. Thank goodness they'd been on Gramps's front veranda—that had totally saved her.

She pushed off the door and headed to the bathroom to splash her burning face and body with cold, cold water. Damn it, she should never have agreed to dinner. She could rationalise her reaction in the car last night as a response to trauma. She had no such luxury tonight. Dinner had been a huge mistake. If she hadn't gone to dinner she wouldn't have seen a vulnerable side to a guy she'd pegged as irritable and difficult. She desperately needed to see him as arrogant, irascible, opinionated, unfeeling and short-sighted, because that gave her a buffer of safety. Only he really wasn't any of those things without good reason and *that* had decimated her safety barrier as easily as enemy tanks rolling relentlessly into a demilitarised zone.

At dinner he'd been the perfect gentleman and he'd walked her home, and—this still stunned her—he'd asked her permission to kiss her goodnight. He was all restraint while she… *Oh, God.* She groaned at the memory and studied herself in the bathroom mirror.

Face flushed pink, pupils so large and black they almost obliterated the blue of her irises, and her hair wild and untamed, framing her cheeks. She looked like an animal on heat. One kiss and she'd been toast. Toast on fire, burning brightly with flames leaping high into the air. Feeling alive for the first time in, oh, so long, and she both loved and feared the feeling.

Why fear it? He kept his word.

And that scared her most because it tempted her to trust again.

'You're looking tired,' Lily said to Kylie Ambrose as she took her blood pressure. 'Are you getting any rest?'

'With three kids? What do you think?'

Lily wrapped up the blood-pressure cuff. 'I think that as tomorrow's Saturday you need to get Shane to take the kids out for the day and you need to sleep.'

'Shane's working really hard at the moment, Lily. He needs to rest too.'

Lily's pen paused on the observation chart and she set it down. 'Shane's not six months pregnant, Kylie.'

'Can you imagine if guys got pregnant? They'd have to lie down for the whole nine months.' Kylie's laugh sounded forced. 'You know tomorrow's the footy so he can't mind them.'

'Sunday, then,' Lily suggested, with a futility she didn't want to acknowledge.

Despite the fact she was both taller and fitter than Shane Ambrose, he was the sort of man she avoided. He reminded her too much of Trent—the life of the party, charming and able to hold a crowd in the palm of his hand, flirting shamelessly with all the women of the town while Kylie, so often pregnant, stood on the sidelines and watched.

'Shane insists that Sunday's family day,' Kylie said in a tone that brooked no further comment. 'I promise I'll catch up on some sleep next week.'

'Great,' Lily said, stifling a sigh and knowing it was unlikely to happen. 'Your ankles are a little puffy so I want to see you next week too.'

'Shane's not going to like that.'

Memories of Trent trying to control her made Lily snap. 'Tell Shane if he has a problem with the care you're receiving, he can come and talk to me and Dr Jackson.' And she'd tell Noah that Shane Ambrose was the one person he didn't have to be polite with. In fact, she'd love it if he gave the man some of his shoot-from-the-hip, brusquely no-nonsense medical advice.

Kylie immediately backpedalled. 'That's not necessary, Lily. Of course Shane wants the best for me and the kids.'

Lily wasn't at all sure Shane Ambrose wanted the best for his family but she felt bad for being short with Kylie. 'If it helps, bring the kids with you to the appointment. Karen and Chippy can keep them entertained while I see you.'

Kylie gave her a grateful look. 'Thanks, Lily. Not everyone understands.'

Lily understood only too well and that was the problem.

Noah heard the click-clack of claws on the floor and turned to see Chippy heading to his basket. 'Hey, boy, what are you doing here on a Saturday?'

The dog wandered over to him, presenting his head to be patted. It made Noah smile. When he'd arrived he'd thought the idea of a dog in a medical practice was ridiculous but two weeks down the track he had to agree that Chippy had a calming effect on a lot of the patients. 'Where's your owner, mate?'

'Right here.'

He spun around to see Lily wearing three-quarter-length navy pants, a cream and navy striped top and bright red ballet flats—chic, casual, weekend wear. She looked fresh and for Lily almost carefree. Almost. There was something about her that hovered permanently—a reserve. An air of extreme caution, except for the twice it had fallen away spectacularly and completely. Both times had involved lust. Both times he'd been wowed.

He hadn't seen her since Thursday night when she'd kissed him like he was the last man standing. He'd thought he'd died and gone to heaven. As a result, his concentration had been hopeless yesterday, to the point that one of the oldies in the nursing home had asked him if he was the one losing his memory.

With a start, he realised he was staring at her. 'You look good.' The words came out gruff and throaty. 'Very nautical.'

She shrugged as if the compliment unnerved her. 'It's the first sunny day we've had this season so I hauled out the spring clothes to salute the promise of summer.'

'As you're here on a Saturday, I guess that means you have a labouring woman coming in?'

'No. I'm here to help you, like I promised.'

Confusion skittered through him. 'But I got the book you left in my pigeonhole and I've read it.' It was a self-help guide that he'd forced himself to read and had been pleasantly surprised to find that, instead of navel-gazing mumbo-jumbo, it actually had some reasonable and practical suggestions. 'Is there more?'

'Yes.' Her mouth curved up into a smile. 'This is Noah's Practical Communication Class 102.'

'I guess that's better than 101,' he grumbled.

'That's the spirit, Pollyanna,' she said with a laugh, as her perfume wafted around him.

He wanted so badly to reach out and grab her around the waist, feel her against him and kiss those red, ruby lips. He almost did, but three things stopped him.

Number one: he was at work and a professional.

There's no one else here yet so it would be okay.

Shut up.

Number two: after two nights of broken sleep and reliving their exhilarating and intoxicating random hook-ups, he'd decided that the best way to proceed with Lily was with old-fashioned dating. Not that he really knew anything about that because his experience with women came more under the banner of hook-ups rather than dating, but his month in Turraburra was all about firsts.

Number three: Karen chose that moment to march through the door like the Pied Piper, with half a dozen patients trailing in behind her.

If he was brutally honest with himself, this was the *only* reason he didn't give in to his overwhelming desire to kiss Lily until she made that mewling sound in the back of her throat and sagged against him.

'No rest for the wicked, Doctor,' Karen said briskly, dumping her bag on the desk. 'Mrs Burke is up first.'

Smile, eye contact, greeting. He recalled the basics from the book. Smiling at the middle-aged woman, he said, 'Morning, Mrs Burke. Glorious day today.'

'For some perhaps,' she said snarkily as she stomped ahead of him down the hall.

'Deep breath, Noah,' Lily said quietly, giving his arm a squeeze before they followed their patient into the examination room.

His automatic response was to read Mrs Burke's history but as he turned towards the computer screen Lily cleared her throat. He stifled a sigh and fixed his gaze on his patient. 'How can I help you today, Mrs Burke?'

'You can't.' She folded her arms over her ample chest. 'Not unless you can pull any strings with the hospital waiting lists.'

'What procedure are you waiting for?'

'Gall bladder.'

'You're—' He stopped himself from saying, 'fair, fat and forty', which was the classic presentation for cholelithiasis. 'How many attacks have you had?'

'One. I thought I was having a heart attack but, according to the hospital in Berwick, one attack doesn't qualify as urgent so I'm on the waiting list. It's been three months and now on top of everything I have shocking heartburn. I feel lousy all the time.'

He tapped his pen, running through options in his head. 'Is there any way you can afford to be a private patient?'

'Oh, right. I'm just waiting around for the hell of it.'

Frustration dripped from the words and he was tempted to suggest she donate to the sarcasm jar.

'I think Dr Jackson is just covering all the bases,' Lily said mildly.

Surprise rocked him. Had she just defended him? Or was she just worried he was going to be equally rude back to Mrs Burke? Ordinarily, he would have said what he always said to patients attending the outpatient clinic at the Melbourne Victoria, which was, 'You're just going to have to wait it out,' and then he'd exit the room quickly. Only that wasn't an option in Turraburra.

Try reflective listening. The self-help book had an entire chapter on it, but Noah wasn't totally convinced it worked. 'I understand how frustrating it must be—'

'Do you really?' Claire Burke's eyes threw daggers at him. 'With that car you drive and the salary you earn, I bet you have private health insurance.'

He wanted to yell, *I'm a surgical registrar. Plumbers earn more than I do at the moment and my student debt is enormous,* but he blew out a breath and tried something he'd never done before. He gave a tiny bit of himself. 'I grew up in a family who couldn't afford insurance, Claire,' he said, hoping that by using her first name it might help defuse some of her anger. 'I can treat your heartburn and I'll make a call on Monday to find out where you are on the surgical waiting list. I will try and see if I can move you along a bit.'

He knew the chance of getting her moved up the list was about ten thousand to one. It frustrated him because the crazy thing was that an elective cholecystectomy was routine laparoscopic surgery. He could have operated on her but in Turraburra he didn't have access to any operating facilities.

You will in two weeks. The thought cheered him. 'Would you be able to go to East Melbourne for surgery if that was the only option?'

'I'll go anywhere.' Claire's anger deflated like a balloon as she accepted the prescription for esomeprazole. 'Thanks, Doctor. I appreciate that you took the time to listen.'

He saw her out and then turned to face Lily. 'You have no idea how much I wanted to tell her she was rude and obnoxious.'

Lily laughed. 'We all want to do that. The important thing is that you didn't.' She raised her hand for a high-five. 'You managed empathy under fire.'

He grinned like a kid let loose in a fairground, ridiculously buzzed by her praise. 'Empathy is damn hard work.'

'It will get easier.' She steepled her fingers, bouncing them gently off each other. 'I do have one suggestion for you, though. Get into the habit of giving the medical history a brief scan before you go and get the patient. That way you're not tempted to read it and ignore them when they first arrive.'

'First I have to show empathy and now you're asking me to take advice as well?' he said with a grin. 'It's a whole new world.'

'Sarcasm jar?' she said lightly.

'I'll pay up on behalf of Claire Burke.' He clicked on the computer, bringing up the next patient history. 'Mr Biscoli, seventy-three and severe arthritis.'

'He's a honey and will probably arrive with produce from his garden for you.'

'It says here he's on a waiting list for a hip replacement.' Noah frowned. 'How long since the Turraburra hospital closed its operating theatre?'

'Five years. It's crazy really because the population has grown so much since then. Now we have a lot of retirees from Melbourne who come down here to live just as they're at an age where they need a lot more health services. The birth centre had to fight hard to exist because we can't push through double doors for an emergency Caesarean section, which is why the selection criteria are so strict.'

Noah leaned over to the intercom. 'Karen, on Monday can you do an audit on how many clinic patients are on surgical waiting lists, please?'

'I can do that, Doctor,' Karen said, sounding slightly taken aback.'

'Thanks.' He released the button and leaned back, watching Lily. He laughed at her expression. 'I've just surprised you, haven't I?'

'You do that continually, Noah,' she said wryly.

'I'm taking that as a good thing.'

'I never expected any less.' She laughed and smile lines crinkled the edges of her eyes. She almost looked relaxed.

God, she was gorgeous and he wanted time to explore this thing that burned so hotly between them. He checked his watch as an idea formed and firmed. 'Emergencies excepted, I should be out of here by twelve-thirty. Let's have lunch together. We can put together a picnic and you choose the place. Show me a bit of Turraburra I haven't seen.'

Somewhere quiet and secluded so we can finish what we started the other night.

Based on previous invitations, he expected protracted negotiations with accompanying caveats and he quickly prepared his own strategic arguments.

'Sounds great.'

He blinked at her, not certain he'd heard correctly. 'So you're up for a picnic?'

Her eyes danced. 'Yes, and I know the perfect place…'

He was already picturing a private stretch of beach or a patch of pristine rainforest in the surrounding hills, a picnic rug, a full-bodied red wine, gourmet cheeses from the local cheese factory, crunchy bread from the bakery and Lily. Delectable, sexy Lily.

'The oval. Turraburra's playing Yarram today in the footy finals.'

Her words broke into his daydream like a machete, splintering his thoughts like kindling. 'You're joking, right?'

'About football?' She shook her head vehemently. 'Never. Turraburra hasn't won against Yarram in nine years but today's the day.'

And that's when it hit him—why she'd so readily accepted his invitation. They weren't going to be alone at all. They'd be picnicking with the entire town.

Lily wrapped the black and yellow scarf around Noah's neck. 'There you go. Now you're a Tigers fan.'

He gave a good-natured grimace. 'This wasn't quite what I had in mind when I suggested a picnic. Tell me, are you truly a football fan or are we here because you don't want to be alone with me?' His face sobered to deadly serious. 'If you don't want to build on what's already gone down between us, please just tell me now so I know the score and I'll back off.'

This is your absolute out. Her heart quivered at the thought. It should be an easy decision—

just say no—but it wasn't because nothing about Noah was as clear-cut as she'd previously thought.

Why are you being so nice, Noah?

Trent had been nice at the start—charming, generous and, unbeknownst to her at the time, calculatingly thoughtful. She already knew Noah was a far better man than Trent. He had a base honesty to him. A man who put his studies on hold to care for his dying mother wasn't selfish or self-serving. A man who confessed to his guilt about finding it so much harder than he'd thought it would be and yet hadn't walked away from it was a thousand times a better man than Trent.

She tied a loose knot in the scarf for the sheer reason that it gave her an excuse to keep touching him. 'I'm a die-hard footy fan to the point that I'll probably embarrass you by yelling at the umpire. And…' She hauled in a fortifying breath and risked looking into those soulful brown eyes that often saw far too much. 'I like being alone with you. It's just that I don't trust myself.'

He caught her hand. 'We're both adults, Lily.

Having sex doesn't mean a lifelong commitment. It can just be fun.'

Fun. It had been fun and good times that had landed her in the worst place she'd ever been in her life and she wasn't going back there. 'That's what scares me.'

'Fun scares you?' He frowned down at her and then pulled her into him, pressing a kiss to her hair.

He smelled of sunshine and his heart beat rhythmically against her chest. She didn't want to move.

He stroked her back. 'Let's just enjoy the match, hey?'

He could have done a million things—told her she was being silly, urged her to tell him why, cajoled her to leave the game and go and have the sort of fun they both wanted, but he didn't do any of those things. She fought the tears that welled in her eyes at his understanding. 'Sounds good to me.'

He kept his arm slung casually over her shoulder as they watched the second quarter and she enjoyed its light touch and accompanying warmth. It felt delightfully normal and it had been for ever since she'd associated normal with a guy.

The aroma of onions and sausages wafted on the air from the sausage sizzle. Farm and tradies' utes were parked along the boundary of the oval and families sat in chairs while the older kids sat on the utes' cabs for a bird's-eye view. The younger ones scampered back and forth between their parents and the playground. She recognised the Ambrose girls playing on the slide and glanced around for Kylie, but she couldn't see her.

The red football arced back and forth across the length of the oval many times, with the Turraburra Tigers and the Yarram Demons fighting it out. When Matty Abrahams lost possession of the ball to a Demons player, who then lined up for a set shot at goal, Noah yelled, 'Chewy on your boot!'

She laughed and nudged him with her hip. 'Look at you. Next you'll be eating a pie.'

He grinned down at her, his eyes dancing. 'I

never said I didn't enjoy football. I may have grown up in New South Wales in the land of rugby league, but since coming to Melbourne I've adopted AFL. I get to games when I can.'

The man was full of surprises. The Turraburra crowd gave a collective groan as the ball sailed clearly through the Demons's goalposts, putting them two goals ahead.

The whirr of Gramps's gopher sounded behind her, followed by the parp-parp of his hooter. 'Hi, Gramps, I thought you were watching from the stands with Muriel?'

'I was and then Harry Dimetrious told me he'd seen you down here so I thought I'd come and say hello.'

'Good to see you out and about, Bruce,' Noah said, extending his hand.

Bruce shook it. 'You seem to be enjoying yourself, Doc,' he said shrewdly. 'I know you'll be on your best behaviour with my granddaughter.'

'Gramps!' Lily wanted to die on the spot.

Noah glanced between the two of them, his expression amused and slightly confused. He squeezed her hand. 'I like to think I'm always on my best behaviour with women, Bruce.'

Gramps assessed him with his rheumy but intelligent eyes. 'Long may it stay that way, son.'

Desperate to change the subject lest Noah ask her why, when she was almost thirty, her grandfather was treating him like they were teenagers, she saw a Demons player holding onto the ball for longer than the rules allowed. 'Ball,' she screamed loudly. 'Open your eyes, Ump! Do your job!'

Noah laughed. 'I think she's more than capable of standing up for herself, Bruce.'

She stared doggedly at the game, not daring to look at her grandfather in case Noah caught the glance.

By half-time the Turraburra Tigers trailed by fifteen points. 'Cheer up,' Noah said. 'It's not over until the final siren. I saw a sign in the clubrooms that the Country Women's Association are serving Devonshire tea. Come on, my shout.'

Still holding her hand, they walked towards

the clubrooms and she felt the eyes of the town on her.

'Hey, Doc.' Rod Baker, her mechanic, pressed his hand against Noah's shoulder. 'You know Lily's special, right?'

Lily's face glowed so hotly she could have fried eggs on her cheeks. Before she could say a word, Noah replied without a trace of sarcasm, 'Without a doubt.'

'Just as long as you know,' Rod said, before removing his hand.

When she'd suggested the footy to him, she'd never anticipated Noah's public displays of affection. Granted, they'd done a lot more than handholding in his car and the other night she'd kissed him so hard she'd seen stars, but in a way it had been private, hidden from other people's eyes. She'd never expected him to act as if they were dating.

Not that she didn't like it. She really did but it put her between a rock and a hard place. If she pulled her hand away it would make him question her, and if she didn't then the town would.

A movement caught her eye and she saw Kylie Ambrose being pulled to her feet by her husband. 'Kylie, you okay?' she called out automatically, a shiver running over her skin.

'She's fine,' Shane said. 'Aren't you, love?'

'Yes,' Kylie said, brushing down her maternity jeans but not looking up. 'I just tripped over my feet. You know, pregnancy klutz.'

'I think I should just check you out,' Lily said, 'Just to make sure you and the baby are fine.'

'For God's sake, Lily,' Shane said. 'You were a panic merchant at school and you're still one.'

Before she could say another word, Noah stepped forward. 'I'm Dr Noah Jackson, Kylie. Were you dizzy before you fell?'

'Kylie's healthy as a horse, aren't you, love,' Shane said, putting his arm around his wife.

'She's also pregnant,' Noah said firmly. 'Have a seat on the bench, Kylie, and I'll check your blood pressure.'

Lily expected Kylie to object but she sat and started pulling up her sleeve, only to flinch, stop and tug it back down before pushing up the other sleeve.

Was she hiding something? Not for the first time, Lily wondered if she should tell Kylie a little something about her own past. 'Did you hurt your arm, Kylie?'

'No. It's just this one's closer to the doc.'

And it was. Two minutes later Noah declared Kylie's blood pressure to be normal, Shane teased his wife about having two left feet, and Lily felt foolish for allowing her dislike of Shane to colour her judgement. She really must stop automatically looking for the bad in men. Good guys were out there—Noah and her grandfather were perfect examples of that—and although Shane wasn't her type of guy, it didn't make him a bastard.

'We still have time for those scones,' Noah said, putting his hand gently under her elbow and propelling her into the clubrooms.

Linda Sampson served them with a wide smile. 'Lily, it's lovely to see you out and about.'

'I'm always out and about, Linda,' she said,

almost snatching the teapot out of the woman's hands.

'You know what I mean, dear,' Linda continued, undeterred by Lily's snappish reply. 'Treat her nice, Dr Jackson.'

Lily busied herself with pouring tea and putting jam and cream on the hot scones. When she finally looked up, Noah's gaze was fixed on her.

'The town's very protective of you.'

'Not really. Have a scone.' She pushed the plate towards him.

'At first I thought all these warnings and instructions were about me. That I'd ruffled a few feathers.'

'I'm sure that's it,' she said desperately. 'But word will get around fast that you've improved out of sight. Claire Burke's a huge gossip and after this morning she'll be singing your praises.'

He didn't look convinced. 'The thing is, the more I think about it, every piece of advice I've been given is about you.' He leaned forward. 'Why is the town protecting you?'

'They're not.' She gulped her tea.

'Yeah, they are, and I can't afford any negative reports about me getting back to the Melbourne Victoria.'

Something inside her hurt. 'I guess we should stop whatever this is, then.'

His eyes darkened with a mix of emotions. 'That's not what I'm suggesting at all.'

She stood up, desperate to leave the claustrophobic clubrooms, leave the game, and leave the eyes of the town. 'Let's get out of here.'

He grabbed a scone and followed her outside as she half walked, half ran, able to outrun the eyes of the town but not the demons of her past.

'Where are we going?' Noah finally asked as they passed through the gates of the recreation reserve.

'Your place.'

CHAPTER EIGHT

THE MOMENT NOAH closed his front door Lily's body slammed into his, her hand angling his head, and then she was kissing him. *Yes!* His body high-fived and he was instantly hard. This was it—what he'd been dreaming about for days was finally going to happen. He was about to have sex again with Lily. He was so ready that he risked coming too soon.

Her lips and tongue roamed his, stealing all conscious thought. Nothing existed except her touch, her scent and her taste. Her wondrous, glorious, intoxicating taste that branded itself onto every part of his mouth. He went up in flames in a way he'd never done before.

She kicked off her shoes and then pulled his T-shirt over his head, sighing as she pressed her hands to his chest. 'I've been wanting to do that for hours.'

He pulled her T over her head and smiled at the filmy lace bra that hid nothing. 'You're gorgeous.'

She seemed to almost flinch and then she dropped her head and kissed his chest before licking his hard and erect nipples. For a second he lost his vision.

'Let's go have some fun,' she said, glancing around. Her gaze landed on the kitchen bench.

'Oh, yeah.' As he moved towards the kitchen his brain suddenly fired back into action. *Fun scares me.*

His body groaned. *Don't do this to me. Now is not the time to start thinking and acting like a girl.*

But try as he might, he couldn't banish Lily's words from his head. *Fun scares me.*

He thought about the time in the car when she'd let go of all restraint and how she was doing it again with such intensity, as if she was trying to forget something.

It was a mistake.

That's what she'd said last time and for some unfathomable reason he didn't want to have sex and then watch her run again.

Why? Usually that's exactly what you want—wish for even. But today it felt wrong. He didn't want to have Lily close up on him again and he knew as intimately as he knew himself that he sure as hell didn't want to be considered a mistake.

He held her gently at arm's length. 'I want so badly to have sex with you right now that it hurts.'

She grinned, her eyes wild. 'I'm glad.'

He stared down into her bluer-than-blue eyes and regret hammered him so hard it hurt to breathe. 'But I'm not having sex with you until you tell me what's going on.'

Panic spread through Lily's veins, pumping anxiety into every cell. She opened her mouth to say, 'Nothing is going on,' but immediately closed it. As much as she didn't want to tell him anything, he didn't deserve lies. Her brain whirred, trying to find a way to give him enough to satisfy him without opening the floodgates to a past she refused to allow back into her life.

She scooped up their shirts from the floor and threw his at him. 'Put that on so you don't distract me,' she said, trying to joke. It came out sad.

He silently obliged and by the time she'd pulled her T over her head he too was fully dressed. She'd hit the point of no return. *Say it fast and it won't hurt so much.* 'The town's protecting me because I was married.'

'You were married?' His echoing tone was a combination of horror and surprise.

'I was.' The memory of those pain-filled twenty-four months dragged across her skin like a blunt blade.

'And you're a widow?'

I wish. Oh, how I wish. She was tempted to say yes, but Turraburra knew that wasn't true. Although only her grandfather knew the full story about her marriage, everyone else knew she'd come home a faded version of her former self and without a husband. She was sure they'd speculated and talked about it amongst themselves, but instead of asking her what had happened, they'd circled her in kindness. 'No. I'm divorced.'

He looked seriously uncomfortable. 'Sorry.'

I'm not. She shrugged. 'It is what it is.'

'Am I the first guy since…?'

At least she could give him the absolute truth to one question. 'Virtually. There was one drunken episode the day my divorce came through but nothing since.' She wrung her hands. 'I'm sorry about my erratic behaviour,' she said, hoping the topic was almost done and dusted because she wasn't prepared to tell him any more. 'My libido's been dormant for so long and you've exploded it out of the blocks. I guess it scared me and I'm really sorry for saying you were a mistake. You're not at all, but you don't need to panic. I'm not looking for anything serious. We can enjoy whatever this is for what it is.' *Please.*

His keen gaze studied her and for a heart-stopping moment she thought he was going to ask her more questions. Questions she didn't want to answer. Information she never wanted him to know.

He wrapped his arms gently around her and

pulled her into him, pressing a kiss to her forehead. 'As much as I find the out-of-control Lily a huge turn-on and sex in a car and on a kitchen counter reminds me I'm not past spontaneity, I want to make love to you in a bed. I want to be able to see you and touch you without the risk of either of us getting injured. I want your first time in a long time to be special.'

She hastily dropped her head onto his chest, hiding an errant tear that had squeezed out of her eye and was spilling down her cheek. *Oh, Noah, why do you have to be so caring?* But before she could overthink things he ran them down the hall to the bedroom.

'Sorry,' he said with an embarrassed grin as he pulled her into the room. 'I'd have made the bed if I'd thought I had a chance of being in it with you.'

She laughed. 'I only make mine on laundry day.'

'But I bet you do hospital corners.' He whipped off his shirt. 'I believe we were up to here when we hit pause.'

She gazed at his taut abdominal muscles, delineated pecs and a smattering of brown hair and sighed. 'I remember.'

'You're overdressed.' As his hands tugged on the hem of her shirt she raised her arms and let him pull it off. 'As much as I love pretty underwear, this has to go as well.' His fingers flicked the hooks on her bra and the straps fell across her shoulders.

As she stood there half-naked in the afternoon light without the cover of darkness, she suddenly felt extremely vulnerable and exposed. She dived for the bed, pulling at the sheet for cover, but it came away in her hand. 'And you don't do hospital corners at all, do you?'

He laughed. 'Obviously not very well but that's in my favour today.' He rolled her under him, gazing at her appreciatively. 'No hiding your beauty under sheets, Lily.' He lowered his mouth to her left breast and suckled her.

A flash of need—hot, potent and addictive—whooshed through her so fast and intense that she cried out and her hands rose to grip his shoulders.

He paused and raised his head, a slight frown on his face. 'You okay.'

'More than okay.'

His smile encapsulated his entire face. 'Excellent, but tell me if something's not working for you.'

He was killing her with kindness and she didn't know how to respond so she did what she always did when she got scared—she took control. Pulling his head down to her mouth, she kissed him, only this time he kissed her back. Hot, hard, sensual and electrifying, his mouth ranged over hers while his hands woke up the rest of her body.

She was hot but shivery, boneless with need yet taut with it too. She wanted his touch to go on for ever and at the same time she screamed for release. She ran her fingers through his hair, down his spine and across his hips. She soaked him in—the strength of his muscles, the hardness of his scapula, the dips between his ribs, the rough and smooth of his skin—all of him. Her legs tangled with his until he'd moved down her body and she could no longer reach them. By the time his mouth reached the apex of her thighs, she was writhing in pleasure, burning with bliss and aching in emptiness.

'Noah.'

He raised his head. 'Yes?'

'As much as I appreciate your focused ministrations, I feel I owe you after last time.'

'No hurry,' he said lazily. 'We've got all afternoon.' He dropped his head and his tongue flicked her.

Her pelvis rose from the bed as her hands gripped the edge of the mattress. 'What…what if I want to hurry?'

'You sure?' His voice was as ragged as hers.

'God, yes.'

He moved, reaching for a condom, but she got there first. 'Let me.'

'Next time,' he grunted, plucking the foil square out of her hand.

'How do you want to do this?'

'I want to see you.'

She cupped his cheek. 'So do I.'

She tilted her hips and with her guidance he

slowly moved into her. Slick with need, she welcomed him with a sob. 'I'd forgotten how good it could feel.'

'Let me remind you.'

He kissed her softly and she wrapped her legs high around his hips, moving with him, feeling him sliding against her, building on every delicious sensation he'd created previously with his mouth and hands. She spiralled higher and higher towards a peak that beckoned. Pleasure and pain morphed together and she screamed as she was flung far out of herself. Suspended for a moment in waves of silver and grey, she hovered before falling back to the real world.

Noah, moving over her, his face taut with restraint and his breath coming hard and fast, finally shuddered against her. She wrapped her arms around him as he came and she realised with a jolt that, once again, he'd put her needs first. No man had ever done that for her once, let alone twice.

It's just sex, remember.

It could only ever be sex.

* * *

Noah's blood pounded back to his brain and he quickly realised his limp and satiated body was at risk of flattening Lily. He kissed her swiftly on the lips, before rolling off her and tucking her in beside him. 'That was wonderful. Thanks.'

'Right back at you.' Her fingers trailed down his sternum.

He drew lazy circles on her shoulder. 'So how long has it been?'

'If I told you that I'd lose my air of mystery,' she said lightly.

Her tone didn't match the sudden tension around her mouth. 'Fair enough.' He wanted to know what was going on but most of him didn't want to lose the golden glow that cocooned them both. 'Let me just say, though, for the record, you haven't forgotten a thing.'

She gave a snort of embarrassed laughter. 'Thank you, I think.'

'I can't believe you're blushing,' he teased her. 'You're a conundrum, Lil.'

Her body went rigid. 'Don't ever call me that.'

Like the strike of an open palm against skin, her tone burned. 'Duly noted.'

She sighed and pressed a kiss to his chest. 'I'm sorry. I just hate that contraction of my name. It's so short that it's over before it's started. All my friends call me Lily.'

He wasn't exactly certain what he was to her or what he wanted to be. Lover? Yes. Colleague? Yes. 'Do I qualify as a friend?'

'A friend with benefits.'

A zip of something resembling relief whizzed through him with an intensity that surprised him. Usually, at this point, the snuggling with a woman was starting to stifle him and he was already planning his exit strategy.

'I need the bathroom,' she said, sitting up with her back to him.

Jagged, pale pink scars zigzagged over her shoulder and across her back. He automatically reached out to touch them. 'What happened here?'

She flinched then utterly stilled.

'Lily?'

'I fell through a plate-glass window. I'll be right back.' He expected her to elaborate on how the accident had happened but she didn't say anything more. He watched her disappear into the bathroom. When she returned and kissed him soundly, he totally forgot to ask.

Lily was pottering around the kitchen, supposedly cooking an omelette—something she did most Sunday nights—only tonight she was struggling to remember how to do it. She was struggling to remember anything prosaic and everyday. Usually by this time on a Sunday evening she had her list drawn up for the coming week, her work clothes washed and ironed, and if a baby wasn't on the way she was ready to sit down and relax.

Not tonight. Every time she tried to focus on something her brain spun off, reliving Noah's mouth on her body and his gentle hands on her skin—and they were always gentle—yet they could make her orgasm with an intensity she'd never experienced. Sure, she'd had sex before, thought it had been good even, and then when everything with Trent had started to change in ways she'd never anticipated—irrevocably and devastatingly final—it had taken the joy of sex with it.

It was a shock to discover she now craved sex with a passion that scared her. To crave sex was one thing—and in one way she was fine with that. What she didn't want was to crave Noah. She didn't want to crave any man because it left her wide open to way too much pain and grief.

Don't overthink this. Like Noah said, it's just temporary and for fun. It has a definite end date in less than two weeks when life returns to normal. Enjoy it and bank it for the rest of your life.

And she was enjoying it. They'd spent Saturday afternoon in bed and then she'd been called in to deliver a baby. Noah had visited the midwifery unit on Sunday morning to do the mother and baby discharge check and had brought with him pastries from the bakery and coffee he'd made himself. Once they'd waved goodbye to the Lexingtons and their gorgeous baby, they'd taken a walk along the beach and ended up in his bed. Again.

Distracted, she stared at the egg in her hand before glancing into the bowl, consciously reminding herself how many eggs she'd already cracked. The ding-dong of the doorbell pealed, its rousing noise rolling through the house. Before she could say, 'I wonder who that is?' her grandfather called out, 'I'll get it.'

A moment later she heard, 'Hello, Doc.'

Her hand closed over the egg and albumen oozed through her fingers. *Noah? What was he doing here?*

His deep and melodic voice drifted down the hall, friendly and polite. 'Call me Noah, Bruce.'

'Right-oh. Come on in, then.' Footsteps made the old floorboards creak and then her grandfather called out, 'Lily, you've got a visitor.'

By the time she'd washed her egg-slimed hand, Noah's height and breadth was filling the small kitchen. 'Uh, hi,' she said, feeling ridiculously self-conscious because the last time she'd seen him he'd been delectably naked.

Now he was dressed deliciously in soft, faded jeans and a light woollen V-neck jumper, which clung to him like a second skin. She swallowed hard, knowing exactly how gorgeous the chest under the jumper was and what it tasted like. 'I…I thought you were studying?'

He put the bottle of wine he was holding on the bench. 'I was but your grandfather called and invited me to dinner. I have to eat so I thought…' He suddenly frowned. 'You knew I was coming, right?'

She shook her head slowly, wondering what her grandfather was up to. In three years he'd never invited someone around without telling her and he'd never once invited a man under the age of sixty. 'Ah, no. Gramps kept that bit of information to himself.'

'If it's a problem, I can go.'

Was it a problem? 'You being here's not a problem but I might need to have a chat with Gramps.'

He rounded the bench and reached for her. 'I'm glad he invited me.'

She stepped into his embrace, enjoying how

natural it felt to be in his arms yet at the same time worried that it did. 'You say that now, but you have no clue if I can cook.'

His thumbs caressed her cheeks and his often serious eyes sparkled in fun. 'It's a risk I'm willing to take. I mean, how bad can it be?'

She dug him in the ribs. 'For that, you're now my kitchen hand.'

He grinned. 'I'm pretty handy with a knife.'

She pushed the chopping board towards him. 'In less than two weeks you'll be back operating,' she said, as much to remind herself as to remind him. 'How many hours away is that?' she teased, remembering his first day in Turraburra.

He pulled his phone out of his pocket. 'Two hundred and ninety-four hours and three minutes, twelve seconds.'

'Seriously? You've got an app?'

He had the grace to look sheepish. 'I was pretty ticked off when I first arrived here.'

'Were you?' She couldn't help laughing. 'I had no clue.'

'And that takes the total of the sarcasm jar to

one hundred and forty dollars.' He got a self-righteous glint in his eye. 'You've now put more money in it than me.'

'That's a bit scary. That jar was for your problem, not mine.'

He gave her a look that said, *You can't be serious.* 'You use sarcasm like a wall.'

Did she? Before Trent, she hadn't been sarcastic at all. Then again, she hadn't been wary and fearful either. The fact Noah had noticed she used sarcasm to keep people at a distance worried her. She plonked an onion on the chopping board to change the subject. 'Dice this.'

'About the app.' He started peeling the onion. 'When I arrived I was taking my frustrations out on the town. I thought I was being singled out from the other surgical registrars and being punished for no good reason.' His warm eyes sought hers. 'It took you to show me I had a problem and that I really needed to be down here. I've hardly looked at the app since our trip back from Melbourne.'

Trent had destroyed personal compliments for

her—she never completely trusted them and Noah's sat uneasily. 'But you must be happy that your time's more than half over. That you'll be back in Melbourne soon?'

'Put it this way…' He slid the diced onion off the board and into her warmed and oiled pan. He stepped in behind her, his body hugging hers, 'I have a strong feeling the next twelve days are going to fly by.'

They settled into companionable cooking—he stood next to her, sautéeing the fillings for the omelettes—and his arm brushed hers as he moved, his warmth stealing into her and settling as if it had a right to belong. He asked her about the music she liked, the books she enjoyed—the usual questions people asked as they got to know each other. It was so very conventional. Normal. Terrifying.

'I've set the table,' Gramps announced, as he walked into the kitchen.

'I'm just about ready to serve up,' Lily said, pulling warmed plates out of the oven.

Bruce picked up the bottle of wine. 'This is a

good drop, Noah,' he said approvingly. 'Might be a bit too good for eggs, though.'

'Never.' Noah smiled. 'I think it will go perfectly with our gourmet omelettes.'

'In that case, I'll open her up.' Gramps, who loved big, bold, Australian red wines, gave Lily a wicked wink before cracking the seal on the bottle. By the time they sat down at the table he'd poured three glasses. 'Cheers.'

'*Salute*,' Noah said easily.

It was a surreal moment and Lily silently clinked her glass against the other two, not knowing what to say. She was struck by the juxtaposition that Trent, whom she'd married, had never sat down to a meal in her grandfather's house and now Noah, who was nothing more than a wild and euphoric fling, was at the table, sharing their casual Sunday night meal. It was nothing short of weird.

Despite her discombobulation, conversation flowed easily around the table and both Noah and Gramps drew her into the chatter. Slowly, she felt herself start to relax. When the plates were cleared, Bruce suggested they play cribbage.

'Gramps, Noah has to study and—'

'I'm rusty, Bruce,' Noah cut across her, 'but, be warned, I used to play it a lot with my father before he got too sick to hold a hand.'

Bruce clapped his hand on Noah's shoulder in a gesture of understanding. 'Tell you what. I'll give you a couple of hands to warm up then but then it's on for young and old.'

Noah laughed. 'That's a fair deal.'

Lily stared at him, once again flummoxed by his thousand sides—so many that he kept hidden from view. With his tailored clothes, his city sophistication and penchant for gourmet foods and wine, no one would ever guess that he loved footy and played cards. 'Do you play other games?'

'Does the Pope have an art collection?' He gave her a grin. 'My parents didn't have a lot of money but we had an annual beach camping holiday for two weeks every summer. If it rained and I couldn't surf, we'd play cards and board games. You name it, I've played it.'

'Me too,' she said, remembering her own childhood summers and Gramps teaching her the card game Five Hundred, 'but I bet you played to win.'

'Of course.' A bewildered look crossed his face. 'Why else would you play?'

This was pure Noah. 'Oh, I don't know. What about for the sheer enjoyment of it and the company?'

He shuffled the deck of cards like a professional. 'It is possible to do both.'

'The man's right, Lily,' Gramps said, rubbing his hands together. 'Enough of the talk, let's play.'

Over the next hour Lily watched, fascinated as the two men battled it out both determined to win. Despite the heady competition and the good-natured trash and table talk, a lot of laughter and fun ensued. It had been a long time since she'd seen her grandfather quite so animated.

To Gramps's delight, he beat Noah by the barest of margins. 'You'll have to come back another time and try again.'

Noah rose to his feet and shrugged into his jacket with a smile. 'Next time we'll play poker.'

Bruce shot out his hand. 'You're on.'

Lily walked Noah outside. 'It was generous of you to give up your evening and play cards with Gramps.'

A slight frown marred his forehead. 'You think I was just being polite?'

'Playing cards with an old man? Yes, I do.'

He sighed. 'Lily, surely you know me well enough to know that I wouldn't have accepted Bruce's invitation for dinner or cards if I didn't want to.'

But that was the problem—every time she thought she had him worked out he'd go and do something totally unexpected. Every time it happened it humanised him for her, making her think way beyond the sexy guy and skilled lover. Making her want to hope.

And that scared her more than anything.

CHAPTER NINE

NOAH STRODE ALONG the main street, eating his ham and salad baguette as he went and enjoying the sunshine on his face. Unlike his first week in Turraburra, when he'd actually sat on a park bench and taken in the ocean view, today he was walking directly from the bakery to the clinic, because his morning visit to the nursing home had run a long way over time.

He'd got distracted with the birthday morning tea for Mrs Lewinski, who was celebrating her one-hundredth birthday. The local press had been there and the staff had put on a party with balloons, mugs of tea, a cream-filled sponge cake and bingo. It was Mrs L.'s favourite game and it had seemed wrong not to stay and play one game with her. He'd lost.

His week had been a busy one—Lily had been

right about word getting out. His third week in town had passed so fast he could hardly believe it was Friday.

'Dr Jackson. Dr Jackson, slow down.'

He turned towards the female voice and saw Claire Burke hurrying towards him. 'Hi, Claire, great day, isn't it?'

'Yes, it is!' Unlike the scowling woman she'd been last Saturday, now she was positively beaming. 'Karen just called me and told me the news. I can't believe it. I really thought you were just spinning me a line the other day to placate me. I never expected you to be a miracle-worker.' She pushed a carton of eggs into his hands. 'These are free-range eggs from my chooks as a thank-you.'

He accepted the eggs. 'You're welcome, and I'm not a miracle-worker. I just made a few phone calls and spoke with my boss at the Melbourne Victoria. I suggested to him that as the hospital had sent me down here to work, it was only right and proper that I finish the work I started. I'll be removing your gall bladder on my first day back in Melbourne.'

'Well, the fact I'll be operated on in eleven days is a miracle to me and I'm not your only happy patient, Dr Jackson. Rita Hazelton and Len Peterken told me their news too.'

Noah matched her smile. 'Like I said, I'm happy to be able to help.' And he meant it.

In his telephone conversation with the prof, the experienced surgeon had been hesitant about the idea of Noah bringing back a patient load with him from Turraburra. Noah had surprised himself at how passionately he'd pushed for the surgical cases. He always saw his surgery in terms of making a difference but, seeing people in their home environment, those differences were even starker.

His life in Melbourne, his income and his access to services had given him a certain amount of immunity to his past. It was easier to forget the difficult stuff but his time in Turraburra had brought back a lot of memories—life in a town without services and hard-working people in low-paid jobs who couldn't afford health insurance. The reminder that he'd lost contact with his roots came with a shot of middle-class guilt and going in to bat for four patients had seemed a valid way of easing it. It surprised him just how much pleasure he was getting out of being able to help.

'We all thought you were a bit of a cold fish, Doctor,' Claire said, her tone bemused, 'but you've totally surprised us, in a good way.'

Thank you? It was time to go. 'It's been good talking to you, Claire, but I need to get back to the clinic. Thanks for the eggs.'

He arrived back to find Lily sitting at Reception with a huge box of vegetables. He leaned in for a quick kiss. 'Are you starting a food bank?'

She laughed and kissed him back. 'Actually, they're for you, along with this tub of honey, a leg of lamb and some filleted flathead. The town loves you.'

He gave a wry smile. 'Claire Burke just told me the town thought I was a bit of cold fish when I first arrived.'

Lily dropped her face in her hands before looking up at him. 'She seriously said that after you've just organised her surgery?'

'It's okay. I know she meant it as a compliment and we both know I wasn't exactly enthusiastic when I first arrived. The funny thing is, Turraburra grows on you.'

A stricken look crossed her pretty face. 'But Melbourne's better, right?'

'Melbourne is without a doubt the absolute best.' He hauled her to her feet, wrapping his arms around her waist. 'Do you want to come over for dinner tonight and help me eat some of this stuff?'

Her brows rose teasingly. 'Cook it, you mean?'

'Well, if you're offering...'

She laughed. 'How about you barbecue the fish and I'll make ratatouille with the veggies. Deal?'

'Deal.' He glanced around and with no sign of Karen or the afternoon session patients he kissed her long and hard, loving the way she slumped against him. 'And just maybe you could stay the *whole* night?'

Shadows rolled across her usually clear eyes. 'It's not like I have a lot of control over that.

Women have a habit of going into labour in the early hours of the morning.'

Only he knew irrespective of a labouring woman, Lily always left his bed before dawn. 'Is it your grandfather?'

'Is what my grandfather?'

'The reason you always leave.'

She spun out of his arms. 'I'm a grown woman, Noah. Gramps doesn't question my comings and goings.'

So why do you leave? He didn't know why it bugged him so much that she did, because in the past he'd always been the one to depart first. In fact, he'd made sure his trysts with women occurred at their place or in a hotel so that he could always make his exit when it suited him. With Lily, staying at her grandfather's house was out of the question so they used his flat. He couldn't say exactly why he wanted her to stay a whole night but he did know that when she rolled away from him, swung her legs out of bed and padded out of the room, a vague hollowness filled him.

An idea pinged into his head—the perfect solution to this problem. 'You have this weekend rostered off, right?'

She nodded. 'Someone's down from MMU this afternoon through Sunday. Why? Do you want to visit that winery I told you about?'

He caught her hands and drew her back in close. 'Better than that.'

She gazed up at him, her expression quizzical. 'Better than a studio room high in the gum trees with a view clear to Tasmania?'

He grinned. 'Yep.'

Her eyes sparkled with excitement. 'Where?'

'My place.'

'Um, Noah, the hospital flat doesn't come close to the accommodation at the winery.'

He shook his head. 'No, I mean *my* place. Come and spend the weekend with me in Melbourne.'

Her eyes dimmed. 'Oh, I don't th—'

'Yes,' he said enthusiastically. 'Come and experience *my* world. Let me show you my Melbourne. We can go to the Queen Vic market for the best coffee in the country, take in the exhibition at the

National Gallery, see a show at the Melbourne Theatre Company, anything you want.'

She stiffened in his arms. 'No.'

The quiet word carried gravitas. He tucked some hair behind her ears. 'Why not?'

'I don't like Melbourne.'

He kissed her hair. 'But you've never had me as a tour guide before.'

She pulled away. 'It's not like I haven't seen or done those things before, Noah. None of it's new to me.'

Her quick dismissal of his idea felt like a slap in the face. 'So you'll spend the weekend at the winery where you've been before but you won't come to Melbourne?'

She shrugged. 'What can I say? I'm a country girl.'

Her dismissive manner was at odds with her usual interest in things. 'Aren't you at all curious about seeing my place?'

She sucked in her lips. 'Not really, no.'

Her rejection flared a jagged, white-hot pain, which burned him under his ribs. *No.* His hand rubbed the spot. It had been a long time since he'd felt something like that and he hated it was back. Hated that he'd allowed himself to care enough to be hurt. 'So this thing between us doesn't extend beyond Turraburra?'

She stared at him, her face filling with pity. 'Noah, you were the one who said sex doesn't have to mean a lifelong commitment. I took you at your word. We enjoy each other while you're here and then we go back to our lives.'

His own words—ones he'd always lived by when it came to women and sex—suffocated him with their irony. For the first time in his life he didn't want to walk away. Lily made him laugh, she called him on his arrogant tendencies and as a result he'd become a better doctor and a better person. She understood him in a way no one else ever had, and because of that he'd opened up to her, telling her more about this life than he'd told anyone.

He wanted a chance to explore this relationship, an opportunity to see where it would take them. Hell, he wanted more than that. He wanted to come home to Lily, tell her about his day, bounce ideas off her, and hear about her day.

I love her.

His breath left his lungs in a rush, leaving him hauling in air against cramping muscles. *No, I do not love her. I can't love her.*

He didn't have time to love anyone, didn't want to love anyone, and he didn't want to feel tied down to another person. Loving meant caring and caring meant his life wasn't his own to do as he pleased.

It's already happened, mate. That empty feeling when she leaves the bed—that's love.

Wanting to show her Melbourne—that's love.

Wanting her to share your life—that's love.

He ran his hands through his hair but the ragged movement morphed into something else. Panic eased, replaced by a desperate need to tell her exactly how he felt. 'What if I told you that when I said all that stuff about commitment I truly believed it, but getting to know you has changed everything?'

'Noah, I—'

'Shh.' He pressed his finger gently to her lips. 'I want to take this to the next level. I want commitment, exclusivity, the complete deal. I want us to be a couple because I've fallen in love with you.'

A look of pure horror crossed her face and she brought her arms up in front of her like a protective shield. 'You don't love me, Noah.'

He opened his hands palms up, hoping the gesture would reassure her. 'It's a surprise to me too but I most definitely do love you.'

'No.' Her voice rose, tinged with a sharp edge. 'You don't.'

Every cell in his body tensed and he worked hard at keeping a leash on his temper. 'Don't tell me—' he immediately dropped his slightly increased volume '—what I think and feel.'

Her face blanched, suddenly pinched. 'Don't yell at me.'

He stared at her, confused. 'You think that's yelling?' He laughed, trying to make a joke to lighten the moment. 'If you think that's yelling, don't come near my operating theatre when a patient's bleeding out.'

'And that's so very reassuring.'

Her sarcasm—her default defensive setting—whipped him, burning his skin. Bewildered, he reached for her, needing to touch her and fix this. How had his declaration of love landed him in emotional quicksand?

She ducked his touch. 'People don't fall in love in three weeks, Noah, they just think they do. You're a doctor. You know about hormones and lust. You've seen the MRI films of the effect of lust on the brain but it's not love.' Her face implored him to understand. 'Think about it. You arrived here angry and disenfranchised, like an alien from another planet, and I made you feel good. You're projecting those feelings onto me but it's not love.'

The logical side of his brain grappled with her argument while his bruised heart quivered, telling him she was wrong. Very, very wrong. 'If it was only lust, I wouldn't be thinking past the next time we had sex or a week from today, but I am. What we have is so much more than sex, Lily, you know it too. I've never felt this way about anyone and for the first time in my life I want to try. We have a shot at a future and it starts with me showing you my real life.'

Her mouth flattened into a grim line. 'I glimpsed it when we spent the day at the Melbourne Victoria.'

'My life's more than just the hospital.'

Her brows rose. 'You're a surgical registrar about to sit your part-two exams. Your life is work and study.'

He immediately jettisoned that line of argument, knowing he couldn't win it, and tried something else. 'I've had the luxury of getting to know you. You invited me into your world and last Sunday, cooking with you and then playing cards with Bruce, was really special.'

'Gramps invited you, Noah, not me. Don't read more into it than country hospitality.'

Her words hit with the force of a king punch and he gripped the reception desk. Something was definitely off. He scanned her face, searching for clues that told him why she was behaving this way. Sure, she had moments of whipping sarcasm but he'd never known her to be so blunt. So mean.

He sighed and tried again. 'All I'm asking is for one weekend, Lily. After all, you've lived in Melbourne so you know one night won't kill you.'

Her already pale face turned ashen and her pupils dilated so fast that the beautiful blue vanished under huge, ebony discs.

A shiver ran over his skin. 'Lily? What's wrong? You look like you've just seen a ghost.'

Her chin shot up and she shook her head. 'I'm sorry, Noah. There's no point me coming to Melbourne with you because we have an end date. My home is here and yours is in the city. These last few weeks have been great but that's all they can ever be. An interlude. We agreed to that and you can't change the rules on me now.'

Incredulity flooded him. 'You're letting geography get in the way of something that could be amazing?'

She folded her arms over her chest, as a slight tremor rippled across her body. 'Geography has *nothing* to do with it, Noah.'

'I know something's going on, something I don't understand. Please tell me what it is so I can help. Whatever it is, together we can fix it.'

She closed her eyes for a moment and when she opened them again their emptiness chilled him. She swallowed. 'There's nothing to fix, Noah.'

'Why?'

'Because I don't love you.'

His lunch turned to stone in his stomach. 'Well, there's nothing ambiguous about that answer.'

'No. There's not.' She wrung her hands. 'I'm sorry it couldn't be different.'

'You're sorry?' Feelings of foolishness curdled with hurt and despair. 'Am I supposed to be grateful you threw me that bone, because, let me tell you, I'm not.' He tapped his chest directly over his heart. 'This hurts.'

Lily heard Noah's anguish and it tore at her, shredding her heart. She'd never intended to hurt him but he wanted more of her than she was able to give. Loving him was too much of a gamble. It would open her up to a huge risk and she'd worked way too hard at rebuilding her life to chance losing everything all over again. 'I said I was sorry.' And she truly meant it.

'Yeah. I heard.' The deep words rumbled around her, vibrating in controlled anger that flicked and stung her like the tail of a switch. 'Did sorry cut it with your ex-husband?'

She gasped as his bitter words spun her back in time. *I'm sorry, Trent. I apologise. I was wrong.* Fighting for control, she managed to grind out, 'This has *nothing* to do with my marriage.'

His expression turned stony. 'I wouldn't know, seeing as you've never told me anything about it.'

Fear and embarrassment rose on a river of acid, scalding the back of her throat. *And I'm never going to tell you.* 'There's nothing to tell. I was young and stupid. I had a whirlwind, high-octane romance with all the trimmings—flowers, chocolates, horse-and-carriage rides and a proposal straight out of a Hollywood movie. I thought I'd found my great love and I got married. Turned out it was neither great nor love, just lust, and it wore off fast. For Trent, it wore off even faster.'

If you'd been a better wife, I wouldn't have had to look elsewhere.

She sucked in a steadying breath to push the memory of Trent's vicious voice away. 'It turns out the affair I discovered he was having was actually his third since we got married. I filed for divorce. End of story.'

His keen and piercing eyes bored through her. 'So you were young, you made a mistake and, just like that, you're not prepared to take a second chance?'

Panic skittered through her. She had to stop him asking questions, digging and probing, in case he got close to the truth. *Do what it takes to stop him.*

Her gut rolled. The only choice she had was to hurt him. 'We're too different, Noah. We'd never work so there's no point trying. Believe me, when I tell you that I'm saving us the heartache.'

'You're wrong.'

No, I'm so very right. 'I have to get back to work.'

'Of course you do.' He swiped his phone. 'Don't

worry. I've only got one hundred and seventy-two hours left in town and then I'll be out of your hair. I'm sure we can avoid each other if we try hard enough.' His generous mouth thinned to a hard line. 'Believe me, I'll be trying.'

With his back straight and his shoulders rigidly square, he walked away from her before disappearing into his office.

As she stood staring at the closed door, desolation hit her and, like an arrow slicing through the bullseye on a target it pierced her straight in the solar plexus. Searing pain exploded into every cell, setting up a vibrating agony of wretchedness. She'd just wounded a good and decent man to save herself.

She doubled over in agony. Playing it safe had never hurt so much.

By Monday morning, back in Turraburra after the weekend, Noah struggled not to hate Lily. He'd spent his two days in Melbourne, preparing for his return the following Saturday. Once he'd lodged the necessary paperwork for the Turraburra patients at the Victoria and booked the operating theatre, he'd concentrated on doing all his favourite things. He'd gone to a game at the MCG, he'd run through Yarra Park, bought coffee beans from his favourite deli to replenish his Turraburra supply, and he'd spent Saturday night at the Rooftop. He'd hated every minute of it.

At the footy, he'd kept turning to tell Lily something, only to find she wasn't there, and later, at the Rooftop, his usual coterie of flirting nurses and interns had seemed bland and two-dimensional. For the first time since arriving in Melbourne six years ago, his shiny and beloved city had seemed dull and listless.

He blamed Lily. He didn't belong in Turraburra but now Melbourne didn't seem like home either.

In his more rational moments he could see that perhaps by telling her he loved her he'd caught her by surprise and rushed her. But it was her reaction to his declaration that hurt most. It was one thing not to love him. It was another to be aghast at the thought and look utterly shocked and horrified by it. She'd looked at him as if he was a monster instead of a deluded guy who'd stupidly fallen in love.

He glanced at the two tins on his desk filled with home-baked lamingtons and shortbreads and at a small cooler that contained a freshly caught salmon—all gifts from grateful patients. The irony was that Turraburra had embraced him. He had more fresh produce than he could eat, Chippy had taken to sleeping under his desk, and the biggest surprise of all was that Karen was throwing him a going-away party. Everyone loved him, except the one person he wanted and needed to have love him back.

He picked up the phone for the tenth time that day, determined to call Bruce and ask him about Lily's marriage—to try and get the real story. He set the receiver back onto the cradle just like he had the nine other times. He didn't have the right to stress an eighty-five-year-old man with a heart condition, and deep down he knew it wasn't Bruce's story to tell.

He thumped the table with his fist. Why wouldn't Lily tell him?

Accept it, buddy. There is no story, she just doesn't love you.

Not possible. But even his well-developed sense of self had started to doubt that shaky belief.

We're too different. He shook his head against the thought as he'd done so often over the weekend. They shared so much in common—love of footy, medicine, sense of humour—the list went on. The only thing they really disagreed on was country versus city living and surely there was a way to negotiate on that? But if she didn't love him there was nothing to negotiate.

The intercom buzzed, breaking into his circular thoughts. 'Yes, Karen?'

'Looks like you might get to do some stitching. Lachy Sullivan's cut his hand climbing over a barbed-wire fence and it's nasty. He's waiting in the treatment room.'

'On my way.' He had ninety-eight hours to fill and with any luck this might just kill sixty minutes.

CHAPTER TEN

LILY'S HEAD ACHED. Her day had started at three-thirty a.m. with Sasha Ackers going into labour. Baby Benjamin, the third Ackers child, had arrived by breakfast, knowing exactly how to suck. From that high point the day had gone downhill fast.

On her postnatal rounds, she'd got a flat tyre in a mobile phone dead zone and, unable to call for assistance, she'd fallen in the mud, trying to use the wheel brace to loosen the wheel lugs. She'd been late back for clinic and had spent the afternoon trying to claw back time, but today every pregnant woman was teary and overwhelmed. She felt much the same way.

The only good thing about the day was the fact she hadn't run into Noah. She wasn't up to facing those brown, angst-ridden eyes that accused her of being a coward. At this point she was just counting down the days until Turraburra returned to being the safe refuge it had always been for her.

All she wanted to do was go home and fall into bed, and that was exactly what she was going to do now Sasha had insisted on an early discharge twelve hours after the birth. Sasha claimed her own bed was more comfortable than the birth centre's and, with her mother minding the other children, home was more peaceful.

Karen had closed the clinic at seven and so all Lily had to do was set the security sensor. As she started entering the numbers a frantic banging made her jump. Someone was pounding on the external doors.

'Hello?' a female voice called out. 'Please, help me.'

Lily rushed to the door, threw the lock and opened it. The woman fell into her arms and she staggered backwards into the waiting room and the light. 'Kylie? Are you in labour?'

Kylie's head was buried in her shoulder but Lily heard a muffled, 'No.'

She automatically patted her back. 'What's wrong?'

The woman raised her head. Black bruising spread across her face like tar and congealed blood sat in lumps on her split bottom lip.

Oh, God. Panic swooped through her. She knew only too well what this meant—all her worst fears about Shane Ambrose had come true. *Safety first. Lock the door. Now!*

In her haste, she almost pushed Kylie into a chair. 'Sorry, I just have to…' Her hands trembled as she bolted the door and started pulling chairs across the doorway.

'What are you doing?'

'Keeping you safe.' *Keeping us safe.* 'From Shane.'

Kylie shook her head quickly. 'No, you've got it all wrong, Lily. Shane wouldn't hurt me on purpose. This…' she gingerly touched her lip '…was a misunderstanding. He was tired and I shouldn't have let the kids annoy him.'

You brought this on yourself, Lily. You only have yourself to blame.

The past thundered back in an instant, bringing fear and chaos. She wanted to put her hands over her head and hide, only she couldn't. Kylie needed her. She needed to deal with this situation. She needed to make Kylie understand that the devil she knew was worse than the devil she didn't.

She kneeled down so she was at eye level with the trembling woman. 'Did he hit you?'

Kylie's mouth stayed shut but her eyes filled with tears.

'He has no right to do that, Kylie. Did he hit you anywhere else? In the stomach?'

'He...he didn't mean to hurt the baby.'

Nausea made her gag and she hauled in deep breaths against a closing throat. *Hold it together. You can do this.* Every part of her screamed to call the police but triage came first—check the baby, check Kylie, call the police. She extended her shaking hand. 'Come with me.'

Like a compliant child, Kylie allowed herself to be led to the treatment room and she got up onto the emergency trolley. Lily handed her an ice-pack for her face then helped Kylie shuffle out of her yoga pants. Two bright red marks the size of a fist stained the skin of her pregnant belly.

Fury so strong blew through Lily taking the edge off her fear.

'Is…is there any bleeding?' Kylie asked, her voice so soft and quiet that Lily could barely hear her.

'Your undies are clean.' Only that didn't mean there wasn't any bleeding. Her hands carefully palpated Kylie's abdomen and the woman flinched. The area was tight. 'Does this hurt?'

'A bit.'

Lily turned on the hand-held Doppler and the baby's heartbeat thundered through the speakers. The heartbeat was way too fast.

'Oh, thank God.' Kylie immediately relaxed, falsely reassured by the sound.

'Kylie, I'm going to put in an IV and call Dr Jackson.'

The woman's face paled. 'Why? What's wrong?'

Lily opened her mouth to reply but the loud

sound of fists banging on the door made her freeze.

'Kylie! Are you in there?' Shane's voice sounded frantic and filled with concern.

Kylie struggled to sit up.

'No.' Lily shook her head as she gently pushed Kylie back against the pillows. Snapping a tourniquet around her arm, she said, 'Stay there.'

'Kylie, honey, I know you're in there,' Shane cajoled. 'I'm worried about you.'

'He's not coming in here,' Lily said, sounding a lot more certain than she felt. She forced her fingers not to tremble as she palpated Kylie's arm for a vein.

'But he's my husband,' Kylie whispered, fear filling her voice. 'I made a commitment to him.'

Hearing the words she'd once spoken tore her heart. She understood the power of strong memories—those of a loving, caring man duelling with the new version of the one who inflicted pain. All types of pain—emotional, financial, sexual and physical—that left a woman blaming herself and questioning everything she believed through a fog of devastated self-esteem. Pain that was *always* followed by recanting, declarations of love and the promises of *never again*.

'Kylie, loving husbands don't put your life and the life of your unborn baby in danger. I have a duty of care to protect you and your baby and that means that right now Shane's not coming anywhere near you.' The cannula slid straight into the vein and she connected up the saline drip.

Kylie slumped as tears poured down her face. 'Th-thank you, Lily.'

'Kylie.' Shane's charming and caring voice was fast developing an edge. 'I just want to check that you're okay. Come on, darl, let me in.'

'I'm scared,' Kylie whimpered, as her hand gripped Lily's arm with bruising force. 'Can you talk to him? Please?'

Don't poke the dragon. 'I'm not sure that's—'

'I know him, Lily,' Kylie implored. 'He won't leave until he knows I'm okay.'

She felt herself caving. 'Okay, but you stay here. Do not get off the trolley.'

Kylie released her hand, nodding her acquiescence.

Lily walked slowly back to the foyer, already regretting her offer. When she arrived at the front doors she didn't open them. 'Shane,' she said, trying to sound calm and dispassionate as her heart thundered in her chest so hard it threatened to leap into her mouth. 'Kylie needs medical attention. I will call you as soon as Dr Jackson's seen her.'

'I want to be with her.'

'I know you do but…*forgive me, Noah*…Dr Jackson wants to see her on her own. As soon as he's made his diagnosis, we'll call. For now, it's best if you go home and wait.'

'You stuck-up bitch.' Shane's charm vanished as he continued to scream at her, calling her names no one should ever have to hear. His poisonous words slid through the cracks in the old building, sneaking under the window seals, their vitriol a living, thriving beast with intent to harm. 'Open the goddamn door now, before I kick it in.'

Lily, you're scum. Lily, you're useless. You're a worthless whore. You ruined my life.

The past bore down on her so hard she gasped for breath, trying to force air into rigid lungs. The edges of her mind started to fuzz.

'Lily, I'm scared.'

Kylie's voice penetrated her panic making her fight back against the impending darkness. *I'm a good person. Kylie needs my help. I have to protect Kylie and the baby.*

Somehow her trembling hands managed to press in Noah's number on her phone.

As his rich, warm voice came down the line, the crack of a gun going off had her diving for safety. With her belly on the floor and adrenalin pouring through her, she commando-crawled for cover under the reception desk.

'Lily?' Noah's voice was frantic. 'What's happening?'

The sound of crashing glass deafened her.

'Get the police. Come to the clinic,' she whispered, barely able to speak against the terror that was tightening her throat. 'Kylie Ambrose is bleeding.'

She left the phone connected, hoping against hope that Noah would use the landline to call the police and keep his mobile connected to hers. That he'd stay on the line and be her lifeline.

He's already your lifeline.

The thought pierced her with its clarity and she gasped. Over the past few weeks Noah, with his love and caring, had brought her back into the world. Noah, who argued with her but never punished her if she disagreed with him. Noah, who loved her but didn't want to control her. Noah, who hadn't run from the hard, hurtful facts that he had a communication problem or blamed her but had worked to change how he dealt with people. How many men would do that?

Some. Not that many. He was one of life's good guys—truly special—and she'd tossed him aside, too scared to trust her future to him because of the fear scumbags like Trent and Shane Ambrose had instilled in her. And for what? A hysterical laugh threatened to burst out of her. She was back to hiding again.

I don't love you, Noah. She shoved her fist in her mouth at the memory of what she'd said to him, biting down on her knuckles to stop herself from crying out in pain. Fear had driven those words from her mouth and she'd do anything to have the chance to take them back.

The crunch of glass under boots boomed in the silence—threatening, ominous and terrifying—taking her back to another dark night and shattered glass. *You survived that and you'll survive this. You have to live so you can save Kylie and tell Noah that you love him.*

The footsteps got closer. Louder. A moment later Shane Ambrose was towering over her with a gun pointed straight at her. 'Next time, bitch, open the bloody door.'

His arrival turned her panic to ice. Now she knew what she was dealing with. Trent had taught her the unpredictability of men and this whole event was all about power. She'd told Shane he couldn't come inside the clinic so to show her he was the one in charge— the man in control— he'd broken in to teach her a lesson. If she wanted to get out of this situation in one piece, she had to do what she'd vowed she'd never do again.

She agreed. 'Yes, Shane.'

He grunted. 'That's more like it. I'm taking Kylie home.'

She kept her gaze fixed on his hateful face and concentrated on keeping her voice toneless and even. 'Kylie's bleeding, Shane. If you take her home, she'll die.'

The gun wavered. 'Don't bullshit me.'

She swallowed, praying that she could get through to him on some level. 'You're holding a gun at my head, Shane. You hold all the cards here, you have all the control. Why would I lie to you?'

'Shane, it's Ross Granger.' The police sergeant's voice, loud and distorted by a megaphone, carried into the clinic from outside. 'I know you're in there, mate, and you've got a gun. We got a call from the clinic saying Kylie and the baby need the doctor. He's here but we need you to come to the door first and bring the gun.'

Shane's cold eyes assessed her. 'Take me to Kylie and don't do anything stupid because I'm right behind you.'

Forcing her jelly legs to carry her, she walked straight to the treatment room. She'd expected the pregnant woman to be sitting up, quivering and terrified, but instead she was lying on her side. 'Kylie?'

Her eyes fluttered open and her hands pressed her belly. 'Hurts.'

Lily opened the IV full bore and checked her blood pressure. It was dangerously low. 'She's bleeding, Shane. She needs a Caesarean section or she and the baby will die.'

The bravado of the cowardly man faltered for a moment. 'Get the doctor.' The gun rose again. 'No police.'

'I have to get in there now, Sergeant.' Noah paced up and down outside the clinic, frantic with worry. 'Gunshots have been fired, there's a pregnant woman who's at risk of bleeding out, a baby who might die, and there's Lily…' His voice cracked on her name. Some crazy guy had his Lily bailed up with a gun.

'Doctor, you can't go in until Ambrose is disarmed. I can't risk any more lives. I've got the medical evacuation helicopter and skilled police negotiators on the way.'

'We don't have time to waste—'

The clinic door opened and Lily stood in the doorway with Shane. He had one of his hands clamped on her arm and the other held the gun pointing at a pale and silent Lily.

'Get the doctor,' Shane yelled.

As if reading Noah's mind, the sergeant said, 'Noah, wait.'

But he wasn't waiting any longer and he bounded forward. Better that he be inside with some control than outside with none. No way in hell was he leaving Lily alone with that bastard. As he approached, Shane stepped back to allow him to pass.

Noah made his second split-second decision for

the day—he decided to just be the doctor and not mention the gun. 'Where's Kylie?'

Shane waved the gun towards the treatment room. 'You have to save her.'

Relatives often said that to him, only they weren't usually holding a gun. 'I'll do my best but I might need more medical help.'

'No one else is comin' in here,' Shane said with a menacing growl.

Noah strode directly to the treatment room. 'Lily,' he said firmly, hating how terrified she looked. He wanted to wrap her in his arms and keep her safe but gut instinct told him not to. Men like Shane Ambrose considered women inferior. Noah needed to keep the bastard on side. 'What's Kylie's BP?'

'Ninety on forty-five,' she replied, her voice oddly emotionless. 'She needs a Caesar but we can't do it here.'

'We don't have a choice,' he said grimly. 'If I don't operate, she dies. We may not have operating theatre conditions but at least we have antibiotics and plasma expander. What about surgical instruments?'

Her eyes widened in momentary surprise before filling with confirmation. 'I can put together an emergency set from the clinic supplies and we have a cautery pen, but I've never given an anaesthetic before.'

'I'll talk you through it. We can do this.' He sounded way more confident than he felt. What he was about to do was combat surgery, only he was a very long way from a war zone. He glanced at the gun. Maybe not.

Calling out instructions to Lily for the drugs he needed, he quickly intubated the barely conscious Kylie. As Lily took over the bagging, he administered the muscle relaxant and that's when reality hit him. They were short one set of hands. He needed another nurse but he couldn't ask anyone to step into this dangerous situation and even if he could, Shane wasn't going to allow it.

He glanced at Shane and the gun. The fact the guy had insisted Noah save his wife made him hope he wanted her to live. 'Shane, can I call you Shane?'

The man nodded. 'Yeah.'

'See how Lily is pressing that bag in and out, giving Kylie oxygen? Do you think you can do that?'

His eyes narrowed. 'Why can't the bitch do it?'

Every part of Noah wanted to dive at Ambrose's throat but he needed the low-life's help and right now saving Kylie came ahead of trying to disarm the creep. 'There's a big chance the baby is going to have trouble breathing when it's born and Lily has the skills to care for it. I'm not asking you to put the gun down. You can bag her one-handed.'

'Fair enough.' Shane sat down at his wife's head and took over from Lily, the gun still in his other hand.

Lily walked over to Noah, her face impassive like she was on automatic pilot. He got the sense she'd gone somewhere deep inside herself to get through this. He surreptitiously squeezed her hand. 'Time to gown up.'

'Time to gown up,' she repeated softly, saying the words like a mantra. 'We can do this. You can do this.'

Her belief in him slid under him like a flotation device, holding him up out of the murky depths of fear. He was operating in a makeshift operating theatre on a woman who might die on the table, a baby who might be born dead, and he was doing it all in the presence of an unpredictable guy holding a gun.

Don't go there.

Panic didn't belong in surgery and as the mask, gown and gloves went on, everything superfluous to the surgery fell away.

Quickly draping Kylie's abdomen, he picked up the scalpel. 'Making the incision. Have the retractors ready.'

A minute and half later he was easing the baby out of the uterus. Lily double-clamped the cord and he cut it, separating the baby from Kylie.

'He's blue.' Shane's panicked eyes followed Lily as she carried the baby to the cot and gave him oxygen. 'Is he alive?'

God, he hoped so, but right now he was battling with keeping the surgical field free of blood and he needed another pair of hands.

'He's got a pulse,' Lily said, relief clear in her voice. 'Come on, little guy, breathe.' A moment later the baby gave a feeble cry.

'That's my boy. Finally after three useless girls I get a son.' The pride in his voice was unmistakable.

Noah almost lost it. He wanted to vault the table and take the guy down. Instead, he bit his tongue to stop the fury that boiled in him from spilling over and putting him and Lily in even more danger.

The baby's cry thankfully got stronger. One saved. One to go. He battled on, trying to find the bleeder in a surgical field awash with blood.

The automatic blood pressure machine beeped wildly, the sound screaming danger and flashing terrifyingly low numbers. He refused to allow Kylie to die. 'Lily, put up another bag of plasma expander, administer oxytocin and re-glove. I need you here with suction. Now.'

A stricken look flared in Lily's eyes as she placed the cot next to Shane and he understood her dilemma. This bastard had caused this mess and now they had to depend on him.

'Please, Shane, will you watch the baby to make sure he doesn't stop breathing?' Lily said evenly and devoid of all the fear that burned in her eyes. 'Your wife and son need you.'

'Of course they need me,' he said, his shoulders straightening with warped pride. 'They depend on me for everything.'

Noah could only imagine the chilling smile that Shane's surgical mask was hiding. The complicated web of emotions that was domestic violence was anathema to him. How could men profess to love a woman and children and yet cause so much damage and pain? If he had his way, after all of this was over, he'd be appearing in court, giving evidence against this man and hoping he got jail time.

First things first. Save Kylie, disarm Ambrose.

The reassuring and tantalising whirring noise of the emergency evacuation helicopter sounded overhead and Noah prayed Kylie would get the chance to use its services.

Lily adjusted the suction and more blood bubbled up.

He swore quietly and cauterised another bleeder. He held his breath. *Please, let that be the last one.* They had limited supplies of plasma expander and Kylie's heart would only pump if it had enough circulating volume to push through it.

The field stayed miraculously clear.

He raised his eyes to Lily's, whose glance said, *Thank you.*

The blood-pressure machine stopped screaming but they weren't out of the woods yet. 'Shane, Kylie needs blood and she needs to be evacuated to an Intensive Care Unit in Melbourne the moment I've stitched her up.'

'And my son?' he asked, his gaze fixed on his newborn baby.

'He needs to be examined by a paediatrician,' Lily said quietly.

'Why?' Ambrose's eyes darted between Lily and Noah. 'Is something wrong?'

'He seems okay,' Lily said, 'but we just like to be thorough.'

'Shane,' Noah said, seeing a potential weak spot in their captor, 'we want your son to have the best medical care possible.

'Damn right. Get over here and squeeze this bag.' Shane kept the gun pointed firmly on Lily as he used the phone to call the police sergeant, demanding that the emergency medical staff meet them at the front doors.

'How much longer are you going to take, Doc?'

'Five minutes.'

Shane put his finger against the baby's palm and grinned when his son's fingers closed tightly around it. 'Strong little beggar, like his dad.'

'Does he have a name?' Lily asked.

Noah's gaze jerked up from closing the muscle layer of Kylie's abdomen. For the first time Lily sounded herself, as if this were a totally normal childbirth scenario.

'Jed,' Shane said.

'A good choice. A strong name for a fighter,' Lily said almost conversationally.

Lily, what are you doing?

'Look, he's looking for a drink,' Shane said. 'Kylie always breastfeeds them.'

Not this time, buddy. Noah struggled with the normality of the conversation. It was like Shane had conveniently forgotten that his violence had put his wife and child in mortal danger. 'I've finished.' Noah set down the scissors. 'Shane, she needs to go now.'

'What about the baby?' Shane asked, still keeping the gun trained on both of them.

'Can you please bring him?' Lily started walking backwards, still bagging Kylie.

Noah manoeuvred the trolley through the wide treatment room doors wishing he could read Lily's thoughts.

'Don't try anything,' Shane said, keeping the gun trained on the both of them as the police and medical evacuation team met them at the front door.

Noah gave a rapid handover, finishing with, 'She needs blood five minutes ago.'

As the flight nurse relieved Lily of the bagging job and the trolley disappeared out the door, Shane grabbed Lily by the arm, pulling her away from Noah. She stumbled backwards.

Noah's heart flipped and he held up his hands. 'Shane—'

'You go with Kylie, Doc. I trust you.'

No way in hell. 'What about the baby, Shane? I thought you wanted him checked out too?'

'Lily knows about babies and she'll do until you send a baby doctor in.'

'I'll be fine, Noah,' Lily said so softly he barely heard, but her gaze—full of love—loudly implored him to leave. To take this opportunity for his own safety.

His heart ripped into two. She loved him. Despite what she'd told him, despite sending him away, she loved him. What should have been the most wonderful news now rocked him with its devastating irony.

The gun moved directly to Noah's chest. 'Get out, Doc. Right now.'

Noah felt one of the police officer's hands wrap around his upper arm. 'Do as he says, Dr Jackson.'

At that moment the baby, who'd been quiet for so long, started to cry.

'Shane, do you want to hold your son?' Lily asked quietly. 'Give him a bottle?'

Shane hesitated, his hand tightening on the gun. Noah, backing slowly out of the door, could see the man's mind working out all the logistics. 'You pick him up and give him to me.'

Lily did exactly as he asked and settled the baby in the crook of his arm.

Shane jiggled his arm to try and sooth the crying baby but Jed, now awake and hungry, wouldn't be silenced. He kicked his little legs, destabilising his position in his father's arm, and Shane, momentarily distracted, moved his gun-holding hand to adjust the baby.

The baby screamed.

Lily moved.

No! Noah watched, horrified, as she slammed the side of her hand into Shane's wrist.

Shane roared. The gun dropped and somehow Lily had it in her hands. Noah threw himself forward, grabbing Shane before he could do anything to Lily.

The police poured into the building, guns raised, and immediately surrounded Shane. Noah relinquished his grip on the man, stepping back as a police officer took the baby and another handcuffed Shane.

Lily sank to her knees, the gun falling from her hands.

Noah ran to her, wrapping his arms around her, holding her tightly, convinced she was going to vanish any second. He frantically kissed her hair, her face and stroked her back. 'You're safe. You're very safe. It's over, Lily.'

Her huge, blue eyes sought his. 'We're…both…safe.'

'We are.'

Her body shook violently in his arms and the next moment she vomited all over the floor.

CHAPTER ELEVEN

LILY OPENED HER eyes, recognising the bright pattern of Noah's quilt. Vague memories of him telling the police she was in no fit state to give a statement and then being cradled in his arms slowly dribbled back.

'Hey,' Noah said softly. 'Welcome back.'

She turned to find him staring down at her, his face full of concern. Despite the fact she'd stupidly told him she didn't love him, despite the hurt and pain she'd inflicted on his heart, he'd never left her side all night. It overwhelmed her. 'What…what time is it?'

'Seven. You've been asleep for eight hours.'

'Gramps?' Panic gripped her. 'Is he okay? Does he know where I am?'

Understanding crossed his face. 'Bruce is fine. He's relieved you're safe and he knows you're with me, getting the best medical care possible.' He stroked her cheek. 'I said I'd call him when you woke up.'

She still felt half-asleep. Her limbs hung like lead weights and her brain struggled to compute, feeling like it was drowning in treacle. 'What did you give me?'

'A mild sedative. I promise it will wear off quickly but you needed it. It was really important that you sleep.' He squeezed her hand. 'Any nightmares?'

'No.' She shook her head and struggled up to rest against a bank of pillows before accepting the steaming mug of tea. 'But I know the drill about nightmares. They'll come later.'

His lovely mouth grimaced. 'The trauma counsellor wants to see us both later today and it's important we go.'

His matter-of-fact words pierced her, reminding her that he'd been through the same awful experience. She squeezed his hand. 'What about you? Did you sleep? Are you okay? You had a gun pointed at you, just like me.'

'I'm okay.' He brushed her forehead with his lips. 'I was more scared for you than for myself.'

She didn't understand. 'Why?'

His incisive gaze studied her. 'Shane Ambrose's vitriol was centred squarely on you.'

'Yeah. He's a misogynist.' She stared into the milky tea. 'You have the immunity of a Y chromosome.'

'And I hated every minute of it,' he said, his voice cracking with emotion. 'I would have given anything to change places with you and when you karate-chopped him my heart almost stopped. You could have been shot.' He stroked her hair. 'Promise me you'll never scare me like that again.'

Tears welled up in her eyes. His love flowed into her like a life force, giving her hope that, despite all her fears, she hadn't lost him. But before she could hope too much she owed him the truth. 'Shane was distracted by the baby and I saw a chance and took it. I had to take it for Kylie and for you. For me. I've spent too many years being scared.'

Worry lines creased his forehead. 'Scared? I don't understand. What you did was one of the bravest things I've ever seen.'

She shook her head. 'That wasn't brave, it was just instinctive survival. I've got a Ph.D in that, courtesy of my marriage.'

His face filled with compassion. 'Perhaps you need to tell me about that.'

She met his warm brown gaze. 'There's no perhaps about it, Noah. There are things you need to know about me, things I should have told you but I was too ashamed to tell you because I've always considered it my dirty little secret.' She licked her dry lips. 'Yesterday, when I had a gun pointed at my heart, I realised I should have told Kylie the story of my marriage weeks ago. I should have told you.'

She gulped down her tea and told him fast. 'You know how I said I'd fallen through a plate-glass window? Well, I didn't exactly fall.'

Noah's skin prickled and flashes of the stoic, non-confrontational Lily from yesterday hammered him, making his gut roll. 'My God, Lily, he pushed you?'

Her gaze seemed fixed on a point on the quilt. 'It was the night I left him. I was stupid. Despite his affairs, despite everything he'd done, I thought I owed him an explanation as to why I was leaving, why I was breaking a vow and a promise I'd made in good faith two years earlier.' Her sad gaze met his. 'But I learned there's no such thing as a rational conversation with an irrational person who thinks that you're his property. His chattel.'

He had the primal urge to kill the unknown man. 'You have nothing to be ashamed about, Lily,' he said, keen to reassure her. 'And neither does Kylie or any other woman in the same situation. These men are sick. Even if I hadn't known that before, yesterday sure as hell taught me.'

'Thanks.' She gave him a wry smile. 'On one level, I knew that Trent's behaviour wasn't my fault but when you're cut off from friends and family, doubt sneaks in and it strips away your self-esteem so slowly that you're not even sure it's going until it's gone. If you're told often enough that you're useless, hopeless, a disappointment, and that everything is your fault, then you slowly start to believe it.'

'Please, believe me, you're none of those things, Lily,' he said gruffly, as a thousand feelings clogged his throat.

She patted his hand as if he was the one needing reassurance. 'I know,' she said softly. 'I truly do.'

'So this Trent.' He spat out the name. 'Please, tell me he got charged for almost killing you.'

'Yes, and there's an intervention order in place against him but I find it hard to trust it. I know that's stupid because he's never once tried to break it.' She wrung her hands. 'Other women aren't so lucky.'

Slowly, things started to make sense to him. Her tension in the car the day they'd driven to Melbourne, her refusal to spend the weekend with him, her accusation that he was yelling when he'd only been emphatic. 'All of this happened when you lived in Melbourne, didn't it?'

'Yes.' Her eyes pleaded with him to understand. 'I met Trent in Melbourne a few months before I started my Master's of midwifery. He dazzled me with romantic gestures, poetic words and gifts. He had a way of making me feel incredibly special, as if I was the centre of his world. It was his suggestion that we elope because—' she made air quotes with her hands '—there's nothing more romantic.'

Her hands fell back in front of her. 'As it turned out, I married him for worse, with two strangers as witnesses in the Melbourne registry office. It should have been my first clue about things to come. How he'd work really hard at separating me from my few friends and Gramps.'

He slid his hand into hers. 'When did things start to change?'

'When I started my midwifery lectures. We'd only been married for five weeks and the first four weeks of our marriage was our honeymoon, backpacking in Vietnam and Cambodia. He resented the time I needed to study. If I got engrossed in an essay and was late with dinner, he'd fly off the handle. Initially, I put it down to low blood sugar and him being tired and hungry after work.'

She barked out a short, derisive laugh. 'I wish it could have been that simple but it was so far from simple it made complicated look easy. The first time I stayed late for a delivery he refused to believe I'd been at work all that time. He called me a slut, told me he knew I was sleeping with one of the registrars, and the more I denied it, the more he accused me of sleeping around. Although I didn't know it at the time, the irony was that he was the one having affairs.

'From that night he insisted on driving and collecting me when I had hospital placements. One night I accepted drinks after work with a group of fellow student midwives to celebrate someone's birthday and he locked me out of the house for two hours. After that, he started to control our money. He took over the grocery shopping and restricted the amount of money I could access to a tram fare. Without access to cash, it was impossible to attend any social get-togethers and if you say no to invitations often enough, people stop issuing them.'

He was battling to make sense of why his strong-willed Lily had found herself in this situation. 'Why didn't you tell someone what was happening?'

'This is the hardest thing for people to understand. I was a small-town girl in a big city with no close friends and in a new course. Every time I got close to making a friend, Trent would sense it and find a way to destroy it.' She squeezed his hand. 'Domestic violence is insidious, Noah. Because your filter is clouded by love and you're not expecting someone who professes to love you to hurt you, you're in the middle of it before you realise. He effectively marooned me on an island of fear.

'I threw myself into study and work and managed to qualify. I was the team member who took on any extra shifts on offer to avoid being at home.'

'But didn't he hate that?'

She gave him a pitying glance. 'Noah, there's

no logic to his behaviour. As much as he hated me not being at home where he could control me, he enjoyed the freedom my absences offered him. He still took me to and from work so he knew exactly where I was. One afternoon I came down with a high fever and work bundled me into a taxi and sent me home early. I found Trent in bed with a woman who had long blonde hair and blue eyes, just like me. She could have been my double. That night I told him I was leaving him.'

He kissed the back of her hand, hating how much she'd been through.

Her voice took on a flat tone as if remembering the trauma of being flung through a glass door was too much. 'I had five days in hospital to think about what I was going to do. The police and the social worker at the Royal helped me take out an intervention order and they even managed to get my clothes out of the flat. As much as I loved working at MMU, the thought of staying in Melbourne was just too awful so I gave notice on the pretext of being homesick. They suggested I apply for a grant for a birth centre to operate down here. I came back to Turraburra, back to Gramps and love, and I slowly recovered.'

Noah's chest hurt from a mixture of pure, hot anger at Trent for his brutal treatment of her and agonising pain that Lily had endured the slow demise of her marriage, her confidence and everything she'd believed she had a right to enjoy. 'You rebuilt your life. That takes incredible resilience and courage.'

She shrugged. 'There were days I thought I couldn't do it but adopting Chippy helped. He's my kindred spirit. He knows what it's like to live in fear. Although no one apart from Gramps knows the real story, the town knew my marriage had failed and they wrapped me up in their care and I concentrated on staying safe.'

'Given what you'd been through, that makes sense.'

She gazed up at him, her eyes filled with shadows. 'I thought it made sense too and I'd convinced myself I had a full and happy life because it was so much better than what I'd had with Trent. It was all working just fine until you arrived and suddenly it was like waking up from a long hibernation and feeling sunshine on my skin for the first time in for ever. You brought me out into the light and showed me what I'd been living had only been half a life. You showed me what my life could truly be.'

Noah held his breath. Since the moment last night when Lily had looked at him with such love shining in her eyes, along with a desperate need to protect him, he'd been waiting and hoping she'd tell him she loved him. Only now he'd learned exactly what she'd been through in Melbourne and on top of yesterday's trauma, which would have brought everything back in Technicolor, he wasn't going to rush her. He needed to give her time and he was going to take things very, very slowly. Take things one tiny step at a time so he never lost her again.

Exhaustion clung to Lily. Telling her story was always like being put through the emotional wringer, but if she and Noah were to have a chance at a future, he needed to know what she'd been through and how the remnants still clung to her. She swallowed hard, knowing what she said next was vitally important. She had to get it right, had to try and make Noah understand why she'd behaved the way she had when he'd told her he loved her.

'All those wonderful feelings I experienced with you both awed and terrified me. Part of me wanted them badly, while another part of me rejected them out of fear.' She grabbed both his hands, needing to touch him, needing him to feel her love for him in case her words let her down. 'Even though I know on every level possible that you're nothing like Trent, me giving in to those feelings felt like I was stepping off a cliff and free-falling without a safety net. When you told me you loved me, I panicked. I said awful and hurtful things, things that aren't true, just so you'd leave.'

She gulped in a breath as bewildered tears poured down her cheeks. 'And despite me breaking your heart, you still came and risked your life for me, Kylie and the baby. I've been so stupid.

I've let that awful secret ruin my chance at happiness with you and I'm so sorry.'

His earnest gaze hooked hers. 'I'm still here, Lily. It's not over until the fat lady sings.'

She gulped in breaths. The time had come for her to put her heart on the line. 'I love you so much, Noah. Can you forgive me and risk loving me too?'

'I love you, Lily,' he said so softly she almost didn't hear. 'That never stops.'

The three little words that had sent her into a tailspin four days ago now bathed her soul in a soothing, life-affirming balm. She cupped his stubbled cheek with her palm, still struggling to understand. 'How can you love me so unconditionally when I've hurt you so much?'

His brown eyes overflowed with tenderness. 'Because you're you. You're a good person, Lily. You're kind, generous and no-nonsense, and, oh, so very good for a grumpy-bum like me.'

A puff of laughter fell from her lips. 'You overheard Karen?'

His mouth twitched. 'I might have.'

She smiled and fingered his shirt, secure in his love for her. 'You can be grumpy from time to time but, then again, so can I.'

'I'm a lot less grumpy than I was now I have you in my life.' He kissed her tenderly on the forehead. 'And talking about *our* life, after what happened on Friday I don't want to rush you into any decisions. I especially don't want to after yesterday.'

Her heart ached and sang at the same time. 'We *both* experienced yesterday, Noah.'

His face tensed with the memory. 'We did and we need to go to counselling so it doesn't hijack our lives. We go for as long as it takes. I want you to feel safe, to feel loved and secure. We can get through this together, Lily. We'll find our way to be a united couple, no matter what it takes.'

His heart beat under her hand—strong, steady and reassuring—and she needed to pinch herself that he was part of her life. This wonderful man who understood that rushing into things was the worst thing for her. 'Taking things slowly sounds like a perfect idea.'

He let out a long breath and she realised he'd been scared she might freak out again at the idea of them being a couple. Her heart cramped and she moved to reassure him. 'Exactly how slowly are we taking this? We can still have sex, right?'

He grinned. 'Absolutely. And do fun stuff together like picnics and visiting wineries and—'

She smiled up at him. 'So we're dating?'

The last vestiges of tension on his face faded away. 'Dating and having sex sounds great.'

And it did. It sounded fantastically normal. 'Lots of good times and wonderful experiences and time to really get to know each other.'

She laid her head on his chest and closed her eyes, feeling his love and warmth seeping into her.

'Lily?'

'Hmm...?'

He wound strands of her hair around his fingers. 'I have to go back to Melbourne in a few days.'

She stifled a sigh. 'I know. You have that pesky exam to study for and pass with flying colours.'

'And you hate coming to Melbourne.'

She bit her lip. She hated that those last vestiges of her marriage, which still clung to her, could hurt him. 'I'm going to get better at that. I know Trent's never breached the intervention order here or in Melbourne and, who knows, he might not even live there any more. I'll be asking the counsellor to help me over this last stumbling block because I want to enjoy being in Melbourne again. I want to feel comfortable there, with or without you.'

'That's great but it's not quite what I meant.' His hand stalled on her hair and hesitancy entered his voice. 'Days off excepted, I'll be working in Melbourne and you'll be down here, delivering pregnant women.'

'You're sounding worried.'

'I know we're dating and I'm fine with that but I'm just checking we're on the same page. I know I said I didn't want to rush you and I don't, but we're an exclusive couple, right?'

She propped herself up fast, resting on one elbow with her heart so full it threatened to burst.

'We are most definitely an exclusive couple. I'll take down any woman who so much as bats her eyelashes at you. I won't allow anyone to steal you away from me.'

His eyes, so full of love, gazed down at her. 'That could be the sexiest thing you've ever said to me.'

She laughed. 'Really? I'm sure I can do much better than that.'

He raised a brow as a smile raced from his lips to the corners of his eyes. 'I dare you.'

She leaned up and whispered in his ear. He sucked in a sharp breath before lowering his head to kiss her gently and reverently, as if he was worried he might hurt her. She knew he'd never intentionally do that and she wanted the Noah who'd made love to her before he'd learned what had happened to her in Melbourne.

Wrapping her arms around his neck, she pressed herself against him, kissing him back hard—needing to feel, needing to lose herself in wonder and banish the past, banish yesterday and everything they'd been through.

He groaned and immediately rolled her over, his mouth and hands loving her until she was a quivering mess of glorious sensation. 'Noah,' she panted, 'now.'

When he slid inside her, she knew she was home. This amazing man was her safety and her security. With him, she could take risks, say what she believed, challenge him, but most importantly she could be herself. As the wave to bliss caught them they rode it together, embracing life and forging a new future.

Later, as she lay in his arms, a peace she'd never known before trickled through her. She knew without equivocation that no matter what life threw at them, if they faced it hand in hand and side by side, they could and would come out the other end not only stronger but together. She couldn't wait to start.

EPILOGUE

'THERE'S PLENTY OF food in the freezer so, please, don't feel you have to cook,' Lily told Karen as she ran through her list. 'Gramps and Muriel are happy to take the kids for two hours tomorrow, which is about as much as they can handle in one hit, but it gives you a break and—'

'Just go already,' Karen said, with an indulgent smile. 'Anyone would think this was the first time you'd left Ben and Zoe with me. Just be back here by five tomorrow or I'll turn into a pumpkin.'

'Who's turning into a pumpkin?' Noah asked, appearing in the kitchen doorway holding a curly blonde toddler and with a pre-schooler whose arms were clamped tightly around his legs.

'Ka! Ka!' Zoe squealed, putting her arms out towards Karen with delight.

'Let's go and see my new puppy,' Karen said with a broad smile as she lifted Zoe into her arms then put her hand out to coax the reluctant Ben to let go of his father's legs.

As Lily watched Karen and the children disappear out the back door she pinched herself yet again to remind herself how blessed and lucky she was. Who would have known underneath all of Karen's pedantic office rules and terse texts there lurked a woman who adored messy children. She turned to Noah, who was at the sink, sponging something sticky off his shirt. 'I've got a surprise for you.'

Noah dropped the cloth onto the sink and caught her around the waist, gazing down at her. 'I love surprises. Promise it involves me having my wife to myself for a couple of hours?'

She stroked the distinguished strands of silver hair that had appeared at his temples. Six years had passed since he'd told her he loved her and if anything that look of adoration that flared in his eyes whenever he looked at her had deepened. 'I promise you it's better than that.'

'How can it be better than that?'

'Well, first of all it's thirty-six hours with me and it's in Melbourne with tickets to that new show you wanted to see.'

His face lit up. 'Are you serious?'

She laughed at his enthusiasm. 'But wait, there's more. We're having dinner at our favourite restaurant and—'

He tightened his arms around her, pulling her in close against him so his heat flowed through her. 'Tell me you booked at the Langdon.'

She laughed and slid her fingers between the buttons on his shirt, her fingertips caressing his chest. 'I booked the spa room at the Langdon.'

He groaned with pleasure as his lips sought hers, kissing her long and hard. 'It's a shame we've got a long drive and we're not there right now.'

'Everything comes to those who wait,' she teased.

He stroked her hair. 'Not that I'm not appreciative of this amazing weekend you've planned for us but now you've got me worried that I've forgotten some important date. I know it's not my birthday or your birthday and it's definitely not our wedding anniversary so…?'

She rested her head on his shoulder the way she liked to do, loving the feeling of being cocooned in care. 'It's five years since you officially became Mr Jackson, General Surgeon, and we polished your new brass plaque and opened the surgical practice in Bairnsdale.'

'Is it?' He ran his hand through his hair as if he couldn't believe it. 'The time's gone so fast.'

Five years ago she'd offered to go to Melbourne to live but he'd been adamant he was coming to join her in the country. 'No regrets?'

'Not a single one. It was the best decision I ever made. With my one day a fortnight at the Victoria I get to keep up to date with the latest techniques, and with my patient load down here I get plenty of chances to refine them. The practice has grown so fast that I need another general surgeon to join me.' His eyes lit up. 'And I just got an email with some fabulous news.'

She tapped him on the chest. 'Don't keep me in suspense. Spill.'

'With the rural medical course at the uni being affiliated with the hospital, you're looking at the new associate professor of surgery.'

With a squeal of delight, she threw her arms around his neck. An aging Chippy, resting in his basket, looked up in surprise to see what all the noise and fuss was about. 'That is so fantastic. Congratulations. I'm so proud of you.'

'Thanks, but it's because of you.'

'No, it's because of all your hard work.'

'Let's agree it's both.' He gave her a quick kiss on the nose. 'All those years ago I thought that being sent to Turraburra was the worst thing that could have ever happened to me but in reality it was the very best thing. I was embraced by a community in a way I'd never experienced in Melbourne and I learned there's something intrinsically special about being able to give back.' He cupped her cheeks. 'And then there was you. You and the kids are what I'm most proud of in my life. You're the best thing that ever happened to me.'

Her throat thickened with emotion as his love circled her. 'And you and the children are the best thing that's ever happened to me. We've been so blessed.'

'We have. And although I love Zoe and Ben more than life itself, they're exhausting on a scale that makes back-to-back surgeries look like a walk in the park.' He grabbed her hand and tugged her towards the door. 'Let's not waste another moment of our thirty-five hours and fifty minutes of freedom.'

She laughed. 'You're not going to set a countdown app on your phone, are you?'

He gave a sheepish grin. 'No need. By the end of breakfast tomorrow both of us will be desperate to come straight home to see the kids.'

'We're pretty hopeless, aren't we?'

He kissed her one more time. ‘True, but I wouldn’t have it any other way.’

And neither would she.

* * * * *

MILLS & BOON®
Large Print Medical

February

Hot Doc from Her Past	Tina Beckett
Surgeons, Rivals...Lovers	Amalie Berlin
Best Friend to Perfect Bride	Jennifer Taylor
Resisting Her Rebel Doc	Joanna Neil
A Baby to Bind Them	Susanne Hampton
Doctor...to Duchess?	Annie O'Neil

March

Falling at the Surgeon's Feet	Lucy Ryder
One Night in New York	Amy Ruttan
Daredevil, Doctor...Husband?	Alison Roberts
The Doctor She'd Never Forget	Annie Claydon
Reunited...in Paris!	Sue MacKay
French Fling to Forever	Karin Baine

April

The Baby of Their Dreams	Carol Marinelli
Falling for Her Reluctant Sheikh	Amalie Berlin
Hot-Shot Doc, Secret Dad	Lynne Marshall
Father for Her Newborn Baby	Lynne Marshall
His Little Christmas Miracle	Emily Forbes
Safe in the Surgeon's Arms	Molly Evans

0116 LP 2P P1 Medical